THE HAPPY VALLEY MYSTERY

Trixie Belden

Your TRIXIE BELDEN Library

Trixie Belden and the
HAPPY VALLEY MYSTERY

BY KATHRYN KENNY

Cover by Jack Wacker

GOLDEN PRESS
Western Publishing Company, Inc.
Racine, Wisconsin

CONTENTS

THE HAPPY VALLEY MYSTERY

Straight to Adventure • 1

TRIXIE BELDEN shook back her short sandy curls, unfastened her seat belt when the light up front flashed off, and settled back in the plane seat next to her friend Honey Wheeler.

"I have to pinch myself," she said, "to realize that in just an hour we'll be in Des Moines, Iowa. It all happened so quickly. Honey, I wonder if I even said good-bye to Moms."

"You did," Honey assured her, "but I wouldn't have been surprised if you hadn't. We were in such a tizzy at Kennedy International Airport this morning—running around claiming our reservations, having our baggage weighed—"

"Waving good-bye to Uncle Andrew," Trixie interrupted. "I just don't seem to remember a thing about the flight from New York to Chicago, where we changed planes. Isn't it thrilling? All the Bob-Whites right here on this plane?"

"Not all of them," Honey reminded her. "I wish Dan could have come. It's the one thing that keeps everything from being perfect."

"All the Bob-Whites" meant Trixie Belden, Honey Wheeler, and Diana Lynch, who were all the same age; Trixie's older brothers, Brian and Mart; Honey's adopted older brother, Jim Frayne; and Dan Mangan, the seventh member of their semisecret club, Bob-Whites of the Glen. Neighbors in Sleepyside, Westchester County, New York, they were students at the junior-senior high school. It was spring vacation, and all but Dan were on a plane bound for Trixie's Uncle Andrew's farm, near Des Moines, Iowa.

"Isn't it thrilling?" Trixie repeated as the plane leveled off and she looked at the ground below.

"No mountains," Honey said, disappointed, "no Hudson River—"

"Maybe not," Jim said. He and Brian sat ahead of the girls. "But, sis, look at the millions of trees and all the fields marked off so exactly and all the different shades of green . . . dark for the woods. . . ."

"Dark woods," Trixie repeated thoughtfully. "I didn't realize that there were so many acres and acres of dark woods. Do you suppose—"

"Trixie Belden," Jim said, "for heaven's sake, let's have one expedition where you don't try to be a detective."

"Why shouldn't I?" Trixie retorted. "If you'll just think back, Jim, you have plenty of reason to be thankful for my 'snooping,' as you always call it."

"That's right, Jim," said Honey. "If it hadn't been for Trixie, I wouldn't have you for an adopted brother."

"I wasn't criticizing you, Trix," Jim assured her hastily. "Most of the cases you and Honey have tackled have finally turned out all to the good. I just hoped you'd have *one* carefree vacation."

"With Uncle Andrew worried about his sheep?" Trixie asked. "How could I forget about it? You know how he hated to go off to Scotland right now. He thought if he postponed his trip for even a little while, he could solve the mystery."

"He had to leave now," Brian reminded Trixie. "He had to be in Scotland this week to complete the purchase of that new kind of sheep, Scotch Blackface."

"You sound like a sheep farmer yourself," Mart called from across the aisle.

"We should at least know the names of the different breeds," Brian answered. "From the time Uncle Andrew arrived at our house, we heard nothing else."

"And ever since we knew we were going to Iowa, I've been studying them," Trixie said. "Jim has, too. We found a good article in the Wheelers' encyclopedia, and more in some old geographies that were library discards we had in the attic."

"Those geographies were so old," Jim said to Brian, "that the girls began to gather up beads and trinkets to use for trade with the Indians they thought they'd find near the farm."

"Well, what if we did?" Trixie bristled. "There *are* Indians in Iowa. There's a reservation near a town called Tama . . . Sacs and Foxes. Black Hawk was one of them. He died there. And, if you please, I know the names of *all* the different sheep there are. So there!"

"Jeepers!" Honey exclaimed. "You really have been studying. I'm not sure I'd even know a sheep if I saw one."

"Remember your Mother Goose book?" Mart leaned across the aisle. " 'Baa, Baa, Black Sheep'?"

"I don't think you know any more than that about sheep, either," Honey said.

"That remark is erroneous and irrelevant," Mart said, "for, while I am not an authority, I am still cognizant of the fundamentals of sheep-raising."

"Isn't he smart?" asked Diana, who sat beside Mart, widening her big violet eyes.

"Maybe so," Trixie answered reluctantly. Mart always exasperated her with his big words. "But what does it mean? I don't think he knows, half the time, what he's saying."

"Maligned, misunderstood, and mistrusted," Mart sighed. "Hey, look at the time! We must be within ten minutes of the Des Moines airport."

Only a week before, Andrew Belden, on his way to Glasgow, had stopped for a brief visit with his brother Peter and his family at their home, Crabapple Farm, near Sleepyside.

Uncle Andrew had never married and was devoted to his nieces and nephews, especially Trixie and the youngest Belden, Bobby, just six. He was the Belden children's very favorite uncle.

When he found his niece and the two older boys at loose ends, it disturbed him. He didn't know that they had spent part of the winter working hard on a successful antique show for the benefit of UNICEF and that they had just staged an equally successful ice carnival for the relief of earthquake victims in Central America. Now spring vacation was at hand, and they were restless; they didn't know what to do with the free time.

The evening after he arrived, Uncle Andrew went with Trixie, Brian, and Mart to a regular meeting of the Bob-Whites. He was amazed at the snug clubhouse, with its central meeting room and the partition where the club's athletic equipment was kept.

"It used to be the gatehouse for our home, Manor House," Honey Wheeler explained to him. "It was falling to pieces when Daddy gave it to us. We've done all the remodeling ourselves."

Trixie had shown Uncle Andrew the big Manor House, just up the hill from Crabapple Farm, with its sloping lawns, stables, and small lake. Diana Lynch's home, just beyond Honey's, was also impressive, for

17

her father was a millionaire, too.

"I like our home best, though," Trixie confided to her uncle. "It may be smaller, and we all have to work hard to help out Moms with the garden and with the chickens, but I never want it to change."

At the clubhouse, as she watched her uncle, Trixie had thought, *He likes Honey. I can tell that he does. And Di, too*—and, as Jim and Dan showed him samples of the posters and handbills they had printed for the ice carnival—*I guess he likes* all *the Bob-Whites.*

"Do you mean to tell me you did all the promotion work for the projects, too?" Uncle Andrew asked. "Printed all these things yourselves?"

"Yes, we did," Trixie said proudly. "It was lots of work, but it was lots of fun, too. I wish we had something exciting planned for spring vacation!"

Uncle Andrew was impulsive. He sized people up quickly. "He never makes a mistake doing it, either," Trixie's father often said.

"Why don't you all go out and stay at my home, Happy Valley Farm, for the week?" he asked. "I'll finance the expedition. You can fly out Sunday morning and be in Des Moines for a late lunch, then be back again the next Sunday and ready for school Monday morning."

"Jeepers!" Trixie exclaimed. "Well . . . well-l-l . . . jeepers!"

"Wouldn't we be an awful lot of trouble?" practical Brian inquired.

"Not a bit. Just the opposite. My hired man has to be

18

away for a couple of days next week, and there may be ways you can help Hank and Mary Gorman, my manager and his wife."

"Gosh, we'd like that," Brian said.

"There are plenty of bedrooms for the girls in the farmhouse," Uncle Andrew continued, "and a lot of room for the boys where the hired man stays, upstairs in the barn. It's snug and warm, with good beds. What do you say?"

"I say let's go!" Honey and Diana said together.

"Me, too," Jim said. "That is, if you really mean we can help."

"I'm stuck here," Dan Mangan said regretfully. "I have to be tutored to stay in the same class with Jim and Brian, and I sure want to do that. It sounds pretty super, though."

"If Trixie doesn't have some sleuthing to do, she'll be sunk," Mart said, roughing his sister's sandy curls.

"What do you mean?" Uncle Andrew asked.

"She's Trixie, the girl detective," Mart explained, "and Honey's her faithful gumshoe companion." Mart then told Uncle Andrew of some of Trixie's escapades.

"That's hard to believe," Uncle Andrew said when Mart had finished. "She's such a pretty little girl . . . so feminine and sort of helpless. . . ."

Mart snorted. "She's about as helpless as a heavy-weight champion," he said. "Do you have any projects she can hope to complete in a week? Any bank robberies? Even any murders?"

19

"You just keep still, Mart Belden," Trixie said. "You think because you're eleven months older than I am that you can always make fun of me. You can just stop it! That's final. Why, Uncle Andrew, what's the matter?"

Andrew Belden's face had sobered as Mart talked. New lines appeared across his forehead, and worry lines showed plainly around his eyes.

"It's nothing," he said, straightening himself. "But you'll be good for the Gormans just now. They've been worried. So have I."

"Anything serious?" Trixie asked.

"It could be," Uncle Andrew said. "You see, for some time my sheep have been disappearing . . . one, two, three—sometimes more—at a time. We always expect to lose a few of them to stray dogs, disease, falls into culverts, or any of the several hazards of sheep-raising."

"And now?" Trixie inquired, her own face taking on some of her beloved uncle's worry.

"Well, it's downright mysterious," her uncle said. "Not a sign of any of the sheep to be found—not a carcass, not a bone or a hair. Missing, gone, disappeared." He spread his hands wide. "Just like that. Not a thing left."

"Not any clues?" Trixie asked.

"Not a clue," her uncle answered. "Oh, well, I'll figure it out when I get back. The sheriff's investigating. You young folks forget about it and have a good time. Happy Valley is a place to have a good time. Lots to do, and much of it will be strange to you. Hank Gorman or Ben

20

will go fishing with you. You can ride the horses, help herd sheep, keep the dogs in order, and eat—eat your heads off. How Mary Gorman can cook! You kids just forget about my worries. Have a good time!"

But the "kids," as he called them, didn't forget about the disappearing sheep. Especially not Trixie. She was just like a bird dog scenting quail.

"I'll simply die dead if Moms and Dad don't let us go," she said, "or if Honey and Di and Jim aren't allowed to go, too. Dan can't, with all that schoolwork."

She soon found that her own parents thought the expedition to Happy Valley Farm an excellent idea, especially if the visitors could help with the work while the hired man was away.

Trixie needn't have worried about the rest of the Bob-Whites. Honey and Jim showed up early the next morning to say they could go. Diana was close on their heels with her parents' permission.

Bobby was disconsolate. He was just too young to go. Mrs. Belden wouldn't even consider it. "I'll just *never* be big," he wailed.

"Never mind," his mother said. "You and Daddy and I will have a wonderful time here."

"Don't want a wonnerful time," Bobby said.

"Circus in White Plains?" his mother suggested.

"Well . . . maybe. . . ." Bobby's face brightened.

Such scurrying about the Bob-Whites did for the next two days!

"Take just as little gear with you as you possibly can," Uncle Andrew suggested. "No fancy clothes. Boots, sweaters, even galoshes. It's been known to snow way into May. Take one pretty dress apiece, girls, for there just might be a dance at Rivervale High School."

So there they were—one day talking to Uncle Andrew in their clubhouse, and a few days later taking off from Kennedy International in New York. Now here they were, fastening their safety belts, ready to land in Des Moines, Iowa.

Slowly the plane lost height, drifted past the busy city, touched down lightly, and taxied up the runway to the airport terminal.

As they entered the building, a short, smiling man with graying hair hurried forward to grasp the girls' hands. He was Hank Gorman, Uncle Andrew's farm manager.

"Say," he said, "I'd have known you anywhere, Trixie." He took her flight bag and turned to greet Diana and the boys. "No mistaking this gang," he said. "We sure are the lucky ones, my wife and I, to have a ready-made family like this for a visit. Our children are scattered to all corners of the continent . . . even got one at the Arctic Circle."

The warmth of his greeting made the Bob-Whites feel immediately at home. He went with them to claim their luggage, grasped two of the bags sturdily, and motioned to the boys to bring the rest. Then they all

22

piled into the big, bright yellow station wagon with HAPPY VALLEY FARM lettered on its side.

Talking all the while, Mr. Gorman guided the car around the circle, out of the airport grounds, onto the highway, and then along Army Post Road, which led to the farm.

Neat clapboard and brick farmhouses, fenced with newly painted white pickets, lined the road. Huge barns flanked the small homes. Long, low chicken houses extended far to the rear. Trees enclosed the shrubbery-circled lawns, and white chickens swarmed everywhere around the trim farmyards.

"It's almost like being at home," Brian said.

"Except for mountains," Trixie agreed. "Whoops! That hill was just like a roller coaster, up and down in a hurry! The trees are beautiful, and here's a river! Jim, isn't it almost like home?"

"It's super!" Jim answered.

For a while they had skirted a heavily wooded area as dense as the game preserve around the Manor House. "Walnut Woods," Mr. Gorman explained. "A good place for you to stay out of. Many a person has been lost there. The other boundary of the woods is the Raccoon River," he went on, "a little high right now and liable to go a lot higher. Then we'll have to watch the sheep . . . not that we don't have to watch them pretty close right now." His face was strained.

"Uncle Andrew told us about the disappearing sheep," Trixie said. "Don't you have any idea at all

23

about what could be happening to them?"

"Not a one. It sure gets me down," Mr. Gorman said. "But don't let it bother you young ones. What's that on the back of your jackets?" He looked at the B.W.G. embroidered on each. "I've heard of New York gangs." He nudged Mart. "You don't belong to any of those, do you?"

The Bob-Whites howled with laughter. Then, sobering, Trixie explained that their red jackets identified them as members of their club. She told him of how they tried to do worthwhile things for other people. "I hope we can help with your work now that the hired man is away," she said.

"I reckon my wife will find plenty for you girls to do in any spare time you have," Mr. Gorman said. "Right down there is Happy Valley Farm. We turn in at the next road."

With a sweep of his hand, Mr. Gorman framed a panorama of beauty. An old orchard ambled down a slope behind the white rail fence that lined the road. In the valley, Happy Valley, Uncle Andrew's pleasant ranch home nestled, a long, low, white-shingled house with green shutters. It extended comfortably across a large yard sprinkled with white chickens and busy geese.

Two brown and white collies ran out, barking a welcome, followed by a huge black cat with fur nervously ruffled.

When the station wagon stopped, Mrs. Gorman came

through the back door, quickly drying her hands on a large checked apron, a cordial smile on her tanned, motherly face.

"There you are, all of you," she said, "safe and sound and back on solid ground." She took the girls into her welcoming arms and patted the boys on their backs. "I've been in a tizzy," she said, her eyes twinkling, "till you really got here. I can't get used to airplanes. I want to feel the earth under me, instead of a mile of air. Welcome, all of you, every one, to Happy Valley Farm. I've a bite of lunch waiting."

"It'll be more than a bite, I'll wager, Mary," Mr. Gorman said, "judging from the dust of flour on your face. You've been baking."

"And glad I am to have young ones to bake for once again," Mrs. Gorman said, brushing the flour from her cheek. "Come right in and make the farm your very own home!"

Black Beard · 2

IT'S A WONDER we could even move after a lunch like
that," Trixie said as she came down the stairs. "Banana
cream pie. Imagine! Mrs. Gorman, our rooms are
dreamy! I have exactly the same flowered pattern in
the curtains in my bedroom at home. I *love* Happy
Valley Farm. See, we're all in jeans and ready to work."

"Indeed, you'll not work the minute you've arrived.
There's a lot more to a farm than work. Wouldn't you
all like to go out and get acquainted with the horses?
Your Uncle Andrew is always talking about the way
his niece and nephews ride."

"We'd love it!" Brian, Diana, and Mart chorused.
"Honey? Trixie? Jim? Coming along?" Mart called back.

"I want to stay in the house and work with Mrs. Gorman if she'll let me," Honey said.

"Not a thing to do, soon as I get through with these dishes," Mrs. Gorman said. "But you just stay here, Honey, if you want to. I'll be glad for company . . . the rest of you, too," she added.

"I was just wondering," Trixie said, "about that crying noise I heard just now—like a hurt animal someplace, sort of far off. Was it?"

"Not hurt," Mrs. Gorman said. "At least, I don't think so. It's a little calf born out of time, and its mother is bawling for it. It's lost. She came right up under our bedroom window last night and bawled, asking us to hunt for it. Betsy's a pet, but sometimes she's a pest. Right now she is. If she'd just hunt hard enough and cry less, she'd find her calf."

"Is that where Mr. Gorman is—hunting the calf?" Trixie asked.

Mrs. Gorman nodded. "He just can't bear it when an animal of any kind is in trouble."

"Would he mind if I went out and helped him?" Trixie asked her.

"Me, too?" Jim inquired.

"Of course he wouldn't. He'd be glad of company, even if he didn't need the help. He's right over the top of that hill, see, south of the farm, in the direction of that big sycamore tree on the slope."

Her last sentence followed Trixie and Jim out the door. After they'd gone through the barnyard fence,

27

they heard the soft tinkle of bells and the baaing of the sheep. Mr. Gorman had told them on the way to Happy Valley that the sheep had been let out to crop the short early grass, after being kept in the barnyard all winter.

They were running from one patch of grass to another, kicking up their heels, shoving, frolicking. "They're acting more as I thought lambs would act," Trixie said to Mr. Gorman when they caught up with him, "instead of grown sheep."

"They're like lunatics in the spring," Mr. Gorman said, "so crazy about anything green they don't know what to do with themselves. Look at those two over there, for instance."

Two ewes, heads down, approached one another, ears laid back and legs stiffened.

"They look just like the good guy and the bad guy walking toward one another on TV. Look at them, Jim."

"Expect them to pull a gun any minute, don't you?" Jim agreed. "Hey, you! You'll get a headache!"

The ewes butted their heads together hard, retreated, approached again, and butted. They repeated the play several times; then, the game apparently over, they separated and began greedily cropping the grass again, not at all disturbed by the spectators or by Betsy's mournful bellowing from across the field.

"Will you let us help you find Betsy's calf?" Trixie asked. She held up her foot. "We've heavy boots on."

"It's a good thing you have. Of course; come along.

Goodness only knows where that crazy calf has strayed. Oh, Betsy, pipe down; we're coming to help you," he called. "Right now I've other business to attend to. Just wait your turn!"

The two collies, Tip and Tag, who had been ranging the hills, came up barking. Tag ran back and forth in front of Mr. Gorman, while Tip ran over the slope, still barking, back to Mr. Gorman, then back over the slope again.

"One of the sheep is down somewhere," Mr. Gorman explained. "All right, Tip, I'm coming."

As he followed the barking dog, Trixie and Jim hurried after him. At the top of the hill, they saw a strange sight. Tip and Tag were circling about a fat ewe who lay on her back, her spindly legs sticking straight up in the air.

"She sounds terrible," Trixie said, watching the ewe struggle, gasping and gurgling, as though she were strangling. "Is she going to die?"

"Thanks to Tip and Tag, no," Mr. Gorman said. "Give me a hand, Jim. There, you take her head, and I'll manage her hindquarters. Flip her over onto her feet. There!"

The poor ewe staggered, righted herself, and, before their eyes, seemed to deflate like a punctured balloon. "They try to roll over," Mr. Gorman explained. "Then their thin legs aren't strong enough to hold them, and they can't get back on their feet. They start to swell, especially if they have new grass in their stomachs, as this one does, and they'd die in half an hour, actually choke to death, if someone didn't help them." He reached down to pat the dogs and pull their ears affectionately. "These boys save a lot of sheep for me."

"There's a lot about sheep-raising we'll have to learn," Trixie said. "I studied it in the encyclopedias, and I thought it was just a matter of turning sheep out to graze, then shearing them and sending them to market."

"Well," Mr. Gorman said, "it isn't all sitting on a hill watching them and whittling. You have to be alert twenty-four hours a day. Even then things happen that you can't understand."

Trixie knew he was referring to the sheep that kept disappearing. *Seems as though* someone *ought to be able to find out where they're going*, she said to herself. *Sometimes stealing goes on right under the noses of people, and they can't seem to see it because they're used to everyday routine*, she continued to herself, remembering some of the experiences she and Honey had had in tracking down thieves. They were going to be sure-enough detectives when they grew up, she and Honey.

"There's that bawling again," Jim said. "Do you suppose that calf could have wandered into the creek down there, sir?" he asked.

"Could be," Mr. Gorman said. "I hope not. It'd mean the loss of a good Guernsey calf, and I can't afford that—right now, especially. All right, Betsy, we're coming. Hi, Tip! Hi, Tag! Go find her!"

The dogs jumped ahead at the sound of his voice and ran up and down the banks of the swollen stream. Soon, from the near side of the stream, they heard a lusty bleat. The collies, furiously barking, rustled the little bawling calf from back of a fallen log. It was hungry. When she heard her baby, Betsy came hurrying to the creek's edge, softly mooing to the small calf to comfort it. It paid no attention to anybody but greedily started feeding.

"Betsy'll get that blamed little nuisance back up to the barn by evening," Mr. Gorman said. "Let's wander back there ourselves. Tired, Trixie?"

"Not a bit," she said. "I love a farm. I love all the animals on it."

"Wait till the week's over, Trixie, and I'll ask you if you really meant that. She just might run into a skunk someplace," he said and nudged Jim.

"I meant I like all the animals that *belong* on a farm," Trixie said and looked back toward the creek edge where Betsy still nuzzled her calf. Across the water, just disappearing back of some trees, she saw the figure of a man. His face, silhouetted against the sky as she topped the slope, seemed covered with a black, bushy beard. *That's strange*, Trixie thought, and she turned to call it to Mr. Gorman's attention. But he and Jim, deep in conversation, were far ahead.

Back in the farmhouse kitchen, they found Honey busily peeling potatoes. Brian, Mart, and Diana were

31

just in from touring the farm on horseback.

The kitchen smelled of sugar and spice and everything nice—roasting chicken and strawberries! "The strawberries are right out of their own garden and into the freezer," Honey explained. "Stop tasting!"

"Shortcake!" Mart whooped. He bent low and smelled the brown crust of the big, round shortcake. "She makes it just the way Moms does," he added as Mrs. Gorman split the crisp brown cake and buttered it. Then she spooned crushed and sugared strawberries over it, gently replaced the top layer, poured the remaining strawberries and juice over it, and set it aside to let the goodness soak in.

"I could eat a stalled ox," Mart said as he moved regretfully away from the still fragrant cake. "Come on, Jim and Brian, off to the shower! Say, Mr. Gorman, that's a snug apartment you have for your help out there in the barn. Warm as toast and lots of books, most of them on farming. I'm going to be a farmer someday."

"It's a good life," Mr. Gorman said. "The books belong to Ben, our hired man. He's taking a correspondence course in animal husbandry. This summer he's planning to go to Iowa State University at Ames for a two-week course. That's where he is now, in Ames, arranging for it. He'll be back tomorrow, I think. Hustle along, boys. Dinner's about ready, isn't it, Mary?"

Upstairs, the girls took out their pretty dresses Uncle Andrew had suggested they take "for a dance," and, as they dressed, Honey and Diana hummed. Trixie, sober-faced and silent, seemed preoccupied.

"What's wrong?" Honey whispered, worried.

"Not a thing," Trixie answered and turned her back to Honey. "Button my dress for me, will you, please?"

"You can't fool us," Diana said. "Something's wrong. Out with it, Trixie. Did Jim say something to hurt your feelings?"

"Of course not!" Trixie denied vehemently.

"He'd never say anything to upset Trixie," Honey insisted. "He thinks she's perfect."

"Except when she's a 'Schoolgirl Shamus,' as he calls her," Diana said. "What is it, Trixie?"

Trixie still insisted there was nothing wrong. But when Diana went to her room for something, Honey whispered, "You can tell me, Trixie. Is it something about the lost sheep?"

"I'm not sure," Trixie said. "I never want to say anything about sleuthing to anyone but you. You're my partner, and we're going to be detectives together. The others just make fun of me."

"What is it, then?" Honey wanted to know.

"I saw a very queer-looking man on the other side of the creek when we were out hunting for the calf," Trixie said. "Honey, he looked like a sheep thief to me."

Honey put her hand to her face to conceal a smile. "Where did you learn what a sheep thief looks like?" she asked.

"All right, if you're going to make fun of me, too,

I won't say anything to *anyone*," Trixie said.

Nothing Honey could say would get another word out of her.

While the roast chicken, mashed potatoes, brown gravy, green peas, apple and celery salad, and an assortment of homemade pickles and relishes were disappearing into hungry mouths, a loud, raucous noise could be heard in the sky overhead.

"It's geese and ducks flying back to Saskatchewan," Mr. Gorman explained.

"There must be a million of them," Brian observed.

"Not that many, but hundreds," Mr. Gorman said.

"We're right on the direct line of the Mississippi flyway," his wife explained.

Their faces were so blank that she laughed. "Tell them about it," she suggested to her husband.

"The noise you hear now is probably blue geese and big Canada geese," he said. "They're migrating. One time four snow geese landed in the field near here to feed. The flyway that crosses this area is the biggest one on the northern continent. Each day at this time of year, we have strange visitors on the ponds, even cormorants and loons. They may stop overnight in the fields, unless the dogs around here start barking and frighten them away."

"I've noticed lots of fat robins," Trixie said. "They're so tame, too. And I saw a cardinal near the spring today."

"The robins are just starting to come back," Mr.

Gorman said, "but the cardinals stay all winter. Almost every bird you can name pays us a visit sometime during the spring migration. On a clear day we can hear golden plovers, flying high on their way from the Argentine pampas to the Arctic Circle."

"Do people do much hunting around here?" Jim asked.

"Not in the spring," Mr. Gorman said. "There's a law about that. I don't think many of my neighbors ever hunt. They don't get much fun out of killing . . . not when so much of their time is spent trying to save the lives of animals. In the fall the birds fly a lot higher, though, on their way south. They seem to sense then that it's open season, with every marsh and pond and stream lined with visiting hunters with lethal weapons. I hate it!"

"Hunting has led to the extermination of some kinds of birds, hasn't it?" Mart asked. "The passenger pigeon is one of them, isn't it?"

"It played a great part in its disappearance," Mr. Gorman agreed. "It's a pity, too," he added. "Everybody finished? Then let's go into the living room."

"You and Mrs. Gorman go into the living room," insisted the Bob-Whites. "We'll get some wood for the fireplace; then we'll all do the dishes."

In spite of Mrs. Gorman's vigorous objection, they had their way. Soon a fire was blazing away, and chairs were drawn around the hearth. Outside, the dogs were restless, starting up nervously at the call of a hound.

"Call them in, will you, please, boys?" Mr. Gorman asked. "They'll startle the feeding birds outside. Anyway, my wife always feels better when Tip and Tag are part of the circle. I'll let them out later, when we get ready to go to bed. They watch the animals at night—or try to," he added with a hint of anxiety in his voice.

Brian went to the door. Tip and Tag came bursting in, stopped at every chair for a pat, then settled down at Mrs. Gorman's feet.

It was cozy and warm around the fire. It had been a long and busy day. They had had to get up very early to drive to the airport. Soon some of the Bob-White heads began to nod.

It wasn't so with Trixie. She was as wide-awake as she had been when Moms knocked at her door that very morning. Her mind was swimming with new impressions and alert with the problem that faced Uncle Andrew and his manager.

"What makes sheep so valuable to raise?" she asked. "People don't eat mutton anymore, do they?"

"It's the only meat that *is* universally eaten," Mr. Gorman said. "In fact, if you were having a dinner for representatives of the United Nations, the only meat you could safely offer all of them would be mutton or lamb. There are no taboos against it, that I know of, such as there are against pork and beef."

"But *we* don't eat mutton," Trixie insisted.

"Without knowing it you do," Mrs. Gorman said.

36

"It's a base for every kind of canned soup. But meat isn't the most valuable product of sheep."

"Wool?" Mart asked. "Clothing?"

"Yes," Mr. Gorman answered, "and fleece lining for coats for men in the armed forces stationed in the far North, for flyers. . . ."

"And women couldn't get along without sheep," Mrs. Gorman said, "for almost every beauty product has a lanolin base—refined from pure wool."

"Hair creams for men, too," Mr. Gorman added. "Do you know a funny thing?" he asked as he thumbed his pipe. "In sheepshearing season, the hands of the shearers are as soft as a baby's. Guess nothing beats sheep grease for calloused hands.

"Then there are buttons, pipe stems, briefcases, diplomas, and twisted peritoneum for violin strings; bagpipes are made of sheepskins, and skins of frankfurters come from sheep's insides," Mr. Gorman continued, "and— Say, Diana's just about asleep. Mart, you don't need to hold back a yawn. No wonder you're tired. Here I've been going on and on. Come, Tip! Up, Tag! We'll go and put the farm to sleep."

"Would you mind very much if I went with you?" Trixie asked. "I'm so wide-awake. I'd love to go."

"Well, then, come along," Mr. Gorman invited her.

"This is Sunday night," Mrs. Gorman reminded him.

"That's right," her husband answered, and he took down the Bible and seated himself in his big old morris chair. He turned to Genesis and read:

37

"And Abel was a keeper of sheep, but Cain was a tiller of the ground. And in process of time it came to pass, that Cain brought of the fruit of the ground an offering unto the Lord. And Abel, he also brought of the first-lings of his flock, and of the fat thereof. And the Lord had respect unto Abel, and to his offering: but unto Cain, and to his offering, he had not respect: and Cain was very wroth, and his countenance fell."

When Mr. Gorman had finished, the other Bob-Whites scattered for the night.

"We'll see first if Betsy brought her calf to the barn," Mr. Gorman told Trixie as he went ahead of her with the lantern. The light threw long shadows dancing around them. Here and there in the valley a dog barked and then was answered.

"That's Ingham's old liver-and-white pointer," he said to Trixie, "and one of the Schulzes' big German shep-herds answering. They've got a raccoon treed some-place, probably, or a possum. Look over there in that corner by the stalls, Trixie."

Curled in deep straw, the little calf lay, its head tucked back along its side. Above it, contentedly chew-ing her cud, Betsy turned a curious head and allowed Trixie to smooth her nose.

Mice rustled overhead, and the tangy fragrances of cows' milk, hay, and corn mingled. Late birds settled in their nests, twittering. Tip and Tag were off to the four ends of the farm. In the moonlight, the white sheep grazed peacefully, some with new lambs by their sides.

"It's beautiful here," Trixie sighed.

"Yes," Mr. Gorman agreed, "and yet. . . ."

Trixie knew what he was thinking. Sheep were disappearing, no one knew where, and all was not as peaceful as it seemed.

A Bad Mistake · 3

THE NEXT MORNING, Monday, the sun was shining brightly. There wasn't a sign of a cloud in the sky, but the air still held some of the sharpness of winter.

The Bob-Whites took turns riding the horses: Diana on Nancy, a gentle gray mare; the boys and Honey and Trixie riding Satan's Baby, a roan firebrand, and Black Giant, a huge black stallion. Nancy was too slow and quiet for anyone but Diana, so Diana lazed along by herself, while the other five took some of the spirit out of the bigger horses.

When the mounts had been carefully groomed and the saddles returned to the harness room, it was lunch-time, and the Bob-Whites went into the big kitchen.

Mrs. Gorman had filled glasses with milk and was putting the finishing touches on a huge tray of choice sandwiches.

"I haven't seen Mr. Gorman all morning," Trixie said.

"He's off mending fences. At least, that's what he intended to do. Isn't he coming in from the barnyard now?" Mrs. Gorman pulled aside the yellow flowered curtain at the kitchen window and looked out. "He's upset," she said. "Something's wrong. I can tell by the way he's walking. Oh, dear!"

Mr. Gorman stomped into the kitchen, washed his hands in a basin near the sink, dried them, pushed his hair back, and sat down at the table in the kitchen dinette.

"It happened again!" Mrs. Gorman said to him.

"Yes, Mary," he answered, "again. Four of them this time, I think. And right under my very nose. Under Tip's and Tag's noses, too. That's one of the things that puzzles me. That and half a dozen other mysterious things."

"You saw no trace of them?" Mrs. Gorman asked.

"Not a trace. Not even a wisp of wool. I tell you, Mary, it gets me down. Sorry, kids," he added as they sat around the table, silent yet sympathetic. "I didn't want to put my burden on you."

"Maybe there's something we can do . . ." Jim began.

Mr. Gorman shook his head and accepted the cup of hot coffee his wife handed him.

"I do wish we didn't have to go to that Farm Bureau meeting over at Rivervale," he said. "I hate to leave the farm, even to drive twelve miles away."

"We can't get out of it now," Mrs. Gorman said quietly. "You're the main speaker, Hank."

"Yes. I have to tell them all about raising sheep. A lot I know about that. Maybe *they* can tell *me* something about sheep-stealing."

Trixie nudged Honey. "We've just *got* to solve this mystery for him," she whispered.

Honey giggled, then put her hand over her mouth. "That's silly," she said. "What do we know about the habits of sheep?"

"We should know something about the habits of thieves," Trixie said indignantly, under her breath. "I didn't like the looks of that man I saw. . . ."

"You wouldn't tell me about him yesterday. You got mad. Tell me now." Honey put her head close to Trixie's.

"What are you two whispering about?" Jim asked.

"Nothing," Trixie answered quickly.

"That's the quintessence of evasion," Mart said.

"If you mean that you think I was telling a fib," Trixie said, "you're wrong. If you mean that I'm not going to tell you what we were saying, you're right."

"Oh, stop arguing, Mart and Trixie," Diana said. She always tried to keep peace. "You're forever arguing about something."

"Well, she—" Mart began.

"Well, he—" Trixie interrupted.

"Please stop your he-ing and she-ing and listen to what Mr. Gorman is saying," Brian begged, his dark eyes serious. He was the oldest of the Bob-Whites, and, whether they would admit it or not, they paid attention to whatever he said.

"Mrs. Gorman and I *have* to go to that meeting," Mr. Gorman repeated. "Just look at the sky! Blue as could be this morning. Not a cloud. Look at it now! Listen to the wind! When Ben called this morning from Ames, to ask if he could stay over a day, I never thought the weather could turn like it has. I'd have wanted him to be here tonight."

"You can't depend upon April weather in Iowa," Mrs. Gorman said, frowning. "If you just didn't have to give that talk! I guess you don't know where to try to call Ben, do you?"

Mr. Gorman shook his head.

"Can we help?" Trixie asked.

"Yes, *may* we?" Mart corrected her.

"Nothing needs to be done unless the weather really gets bad," Mr. Gorman said.

"If it does turn bad, does something need to be done before you get back?" Trixie asked.

"If it should start to snow—"

"*Snow*," Trixie repeated, surprised.

"It just could, you know," Mr. Gorman went on. "The sky looks pretty threatening right now. If it should snow," he said thoughtfully, "then the sheep would have to be put in the field where the shelters are."

"We can do that, sir," Jim said.

"I'd do it myself," Mr. Gorman said, "but there isn't time. Tip and Tag can really manage, but, smart as they are, they're still just dogs. They have to have some human direction. Did you have any trouble with the horses when you took them out to exercise them?"

"That Nancy is the gentlest horse I ever rode," Diana said. "I love her."

"She's old," Mrs. Gorman said. "She's my pet. We've had her a long time."

"How about Satan's Baby and Black Giant?" Mr. Gorman asked, smiling. "You can't call them gentle."

"They didn't give us any trouble," Trixie said. "You should just take a run on some of the horses in Honey's father's stable. I had one ride I'll never forget."

"Satan's Baby and Black Giant can almost turn the sheep into the field themselves if it needs to be done," Mr. Gorman said. "I do wish I didn't have to go."

"Right now most of the flock is staying pretty close to home," Mrs. Gorman said, "right down there grazing in the field near the barns."

"That's right," Mr. Gorman said. "You probably won't need the horses at all—just Tip and Tag. Want to go out now for a quick look around?" he asked. "I'll show you what has to be done if a storm comes up. You won't have any trouble."

Trixie went with Mr. Gorman and the boys. Honey and Diana stayed behind to help Mrs. Gorman, who insisted on having the dinner all ready for the Bob-

Whites before she would dress to go to Rivervale with her husband. "All you have to do, then," she said, "is put it in the oven and warm it."

The sky was still dark, and big clouds had rolled in from the northwest as Mr. and Mrs. Gorman drove out of the yard.

"We'll take care of everything. Don't you worry," Trixie called after them.

"If he only knew some of the tight places we've been in and managed to squeeze out of," Honey said.

"Yes," Trixie agreed. "The time, for instance, that Jim's stepfather set fire to Jim's uncle's old mansion."

"And you were the one who saved Jim's half-million-dollar inheritance, and I acquired a darling redheaded brother when Mother and Daddy adopted Jim!"

Trixie blushed. "I just can't remember what our lives were like without Jim," she said.

"Your life, especially," Mart teased. "I guess we've really run down some tough customers, haven't we?"

"What do you mean 'we'?" Trixie asked, turning to face Mart. "Honey and I . . . we were the detectives. You just made fun of us till we'd solved the mysteries, and then you claimed some of the credit."

"Yeah? You'd never have escaped from that stolen trailer if it hadn't been for me. You're just jealous of my superior deductive instincts," Mart said.

"There you go again, talking gobbledygook," Trixie said. "Honestly, though, Mart," she added, ashamed

45

of herself, "you always have been a big help, hasn't he, Honey?"

"Of course he has," Honey agreed, "and Brian and Jim have, too, especially the time when you were marooned all night in the blizzard."

"I guess a little thing like an Iowa snow needn't worry us any after that," Jim said.

"Holy cow, look at those flakes," Mart called from the window. "Iowa snow or New York snow, it sure is coming down."

Trixie ran to the window, then turned to the other Bob-Whites. "We'd better get busy," she said, "and in a hurry, too. Come on!"

Outside, Brian whistled to Tip and Tag, who were up in the apple orchard chasing the big flakes as they swirled to the ground.

"Come along!" he said to the dogs. Then he called to the girls, "Go on back in the house and get dinner ready. Warm up the things Mrs. Gorman left. We'll take care of this."

Obediently, Honey and Diana turned back—but not Trixie.

"You can't order me around like that, Brian Belden," she said. "Jeepers, just look at the way that snow is coming down . . . like closed fists!"

"It's wet and wadded together," Jim said. "It's almost covered the ground already."

"And the sheep," Trixie said. "Don't they look queer? They have topcoats of snow wool. How was it that Mr.

Gorman said to call them last night?"

"I know," Jim said. "It sounded something like an auctioneer's lingo."

"Suppose you call them, then," Brian suggested, "before Tip and Tag scatter them all over the landscape. What's the matter with those crazy dogs, anyway?"

Trixie whistled and called, "Here, Tag! Here, Tip!" and the dogs obeyed. "Someone tell them what to do," she said. "Jim, call the sheep!"

Jim cupped his hands around his mouth. "Sooooo—sheep!" he called. The Beldens doubled up, laughing. "Hush!" Jim said. "Ooooo—baaaa—aaaa! Sooooo—sheep!"

It must not have sounded funny to the sheep, even if it did to the Bob-Whites, for their heads went up, and when two big ewes started toward Jim's voice, the rest obediently followed.

The boys went out into the field then, to run ahead of the sheep toward the shelter field. "After them, Tip!" Trixie called. "Good boy, Tag!" Heads up, barking, their tails going like semaphores, the dogs ran back and forth, circling always, herding the sheep into a smaller area, directing them toward the shelters.

"Tip's gone astray after something," Mart called as one of the collies disappeared over the top of a knoll. "After a cottontail, I'll bet. The snow brings them out. I wish he'd keep his mind on the business at hand. Where does he think he's going?"

"Let him alone. The sheep are all going through the

gate now," Trixie said. Then, as she caught sight of Tip, she shouted, "There he is now. See what he found!"

Over the knoll, urged ahead by the circling collie, came two young ewes, protesting angrily.

"Tip knows more than a person does," Brian said. "There goes Tag now."

After half a dozen such forays, the dogs seemed to be content. "They're so smart," Mart said. "I believe they can even count, and they know that now the flock's all in and safe."

It seemed so, indeed, for the collies watched Jim and Brian pull the gate shut, saw the sheep seek shelter under the roofed sheds, then followed the Bob-Whites back to the house.

They were just inside when the telephone rang. Diana answered. "Yes, Mr. Gorman. Oh, yes, everything's fine. The boys and Trixie just came in. Here's Brian. Do you want to speak to him?"

They all listened to Mr. Gorman's voice. It sounded strained at first. They couldn't hear what he was saying to Brian, but Trixie gave a sigh of relief as the manager's voice softened and seemed less worried when Brian told him the sheep were all under shelter.

"It wasn't any too soon," Trixie sighed. "The snow must be two inches deep now. No wonder Mr. Gorman was worried. It's still snowing. It doesn't snow big wet wads of flakes like this in Sleepyside, does it?"

"Let's forget Sleepyside for the moment," Mart suggested. "Say, Di, something smells wonderful! After dinner let's watch TV, shall we?"

"With that table tennis set in the basement? Not me!" Jim said. "Let's pair up. Trixie and I'll take you all on in turns."

"Mrs. Gorman said there's an old record player in the playroom," Honey said, "and some records more than twenty years old. She thought we'd have a ball playing them."

"Twenty years old . . . gosh!" Trixie said. "I didn't even know they made records that long ago. It'll probably be one of those old machines with a big horn. You know . . . someone gave us one to sell at our antique show for UNICEF."

"It's not that ancient. I saw it," Brian said. "Jiminy, Trixie, you'd think twenty years ago was the Dark Ages. They had pretty slick songs then. Dick Drake and his gang sing some of them now."

"And I think they're cute," Honey said. "Come on, let's have our dinner now. Di actually made some corn bread!"

"It was a mix," Diana said modestly. "For the rest of the dinner, Mrs. Gorman had a thick slice of ham ready to go into the oven. She puts mustard and pine-apple juice and—"

"The more glop you put on ham, the better I like it," Mart said. "What's keeping us?"

"Washing your hands, for one thing," Trixie said. "Mart, hurry up, 'cause there's apple pie for dessert."

While they were eating, Tip and Tag didn't seem able

to settle down, though they had eaten their food eagerly when Trixie gave it to them. They ran in and out of the dining room, back and forth to the back door, whining restlessly.

"What do you think is wrong with the dogs?" Trixie asked. "If it weren't storming so hard, I'd think we should let them out to run."

"It's the wind that bothers them," Mart said. "Dogs don't like wind."

"I don't like it, either," Trixie said. "I'm glad the sheep are all safe and that we could do at least that much to help the Gormans."

"They're surely wonderful to us," Honey said. "I'm glad, too, that you could help."

When Mr. and Mrs. Gorman returned, the Bob-Whites didn't hear them at first. The record player was going full blast, and Diana and Mart were trying to do the Charleston the way they'd seen it done on television.

As a lull came in the music, they heard Mrs. Gorman's footsteps overhead, so they all crowded up the stairs.

"Did you have a good time?" Honey asked.

"Is the storm still bad?" Trixie asked. "Why, Mrs. Gorman, what *is* the matter? Where is Mr. Gorman?"

"Out in the snow, that's where he is," Mrs. Gorman said, near tears. "Oh, why couldn't you have been depended upon to do a little thing like putting the sheep under shelter? Why did you tell him it had been done when it hadn't? How could you?"

"But it *was* done," Trixie said. "We *did* do it. We really did. All Mr. Gorman has to do is to go out there and look, and he'll find the sheep safe and sound in the shelter field. We put them there, Mrs. Gorman. I helped the boys pull the gate shut after them—"

"And lock it?" Mrs. Gorman asked. "Did you drop the wooden bar down to lock it?"

Trixie's face fell. Jim's, too. And Brian's. There was a moment of silence.

"Uh-oh," Mart groaned.

"No, Mrs. Gorman," Trixie said sadly, "we didn't. I guess we didn't know. The dogs knew, though. They have been sort of frantic . . . running to the door, then back to us. No, we didn't lock the gate. Are the sheep all gone, every one of them?"

"Every one," Mrs. Gorman said and sank into a chair. "Heaven knows where they are. They'll be frozen or smothered, and Hank'll lose half the herd and his job, too, what with all the stolen sheep. Where are you going?" she called.

"Out to help," said the Bob-Whites. They struggled into their coats, pulled on galoshes, and were gone out the door, Trixie ahead of them with a big flashlight. "We've been in worse mix-ups than this," she said to the others. "And we've gotten out of them. This'll turn out all right, too. See if it doesn't."

The Trapped Sheep · 4

THE FLOODLIGHTS in the farmyard were turned on, but only a faint blob of light showed, so dense was the falling snow. Betsy's small calf, startled by all the noise, bawled mournfully. Everywhere else there was a silence . . . not a tinkle of a sheep's bell, not a sound of Tip's or Tag's barking. The Bob-Whites had no idea where Mr. Gorman was.

"It's a good thing we rode around the farm today," Jim said. "At least we know something of the layout, but I still don't know which direction we should take first."

"If you were a sheep in a snowstorm, where would you go?" Mart asked.

"Isn't he crazy?" Diana said. "He finds fun in everything." No one else seemed to think it was time for fun.

"Well, it isn't a funeral, you know," Mart said and balled some snow and threw it at Trixie, who struggled far ahead.

"Stop fooling!" Trixie turned around to say. "It may very well *be* a funeral . . . the funeral of a lot of Uncle Andrew's sheep. And it's all our fault. I wish we could find Mr. Gorman."

"I don't know why the dumb sheep wouldn't stay under the shelters without having to be made to do it," Mart said. "Is that one of the dogs barking?"

Snuffling noisily, Tip appeared out of the curtain of thick snow. Half whining, half barking, he wiggled his wet body against Brian's legs, then dashed off into nowhere. The Bob-Whites followed his whimpering up a hillock, their flashlights barely cutting the darkness ahead. As they topped the hill, they could discern the blurred light of Mr. Gorman's big flash lantern.

As the Bob-Whites appeared, Trixie leading the way, Mr. Gorman's recognition of them was anything but cordial.

"You'd better get right back to the house," he said. "I have enough on my mind, trying to find the sheep. I don't want a bunch of lost kids as well. If you turn back now, you can follow your own footprints. I'd appreciate it if you'd please go back."

"It's no wonder he's angry with us," Trixie said under her breath to Jim. "But I'll tell you one thing:

53

I'm not going back till those sheep are found.

"Mr. Gorman," she called, "you haven't located any of the sheep, have you?"

"I haven't," he answered. "But Tip and Tag have. They sound as though they've found them in the edge of the woods over the hill."

"All of them?" Trixie asked.

"How can I tell that until I catch up with them?" he asked, irritated. "You'd do me a big favor, all of you, if you'd just go on back to the house. You've done—"

"I know," Trixie said. "We've done enough damage for one day. The dogs seem to be heading the sheep this way, don't they?"

"They do. Keep out of the way, please, or you'll be knocked over," Mr. Gorman called as he urged the dogs out in circles to drive the sheep toward the shelter field.

The Bob-Whites ran to one side of the milling animals as half a dozen old ewes led and the others followed, running ahead of the yapping dogs.

"About all we seem to be able to do is to make things tougher for Mr. Gorman," Brian said. "We might as well go back," he added dejectedly. "Say, Jim, I can't believe that's all the flock, can you? Can you, Trixie? If that's over two hundred sheep, they're surely making better time now than they did when we put them in the shelter field."

"It isn't all of them," Trixie said, "and Tip knows it. Listen to him!"

Tip, following Mr. Gorman's sharp command to him and to Tag, circled the wet mass of sheep and drove them on. Now and then, however, he ran back to where the Bob-Whites waited. He jumped up to pull at Trixie's sleeve, ran off into the blurred half-light of the snow, then ran back again to rub his wet body against Jim's jeans.

"That dog is trying to tell someone something," Honey said. "Mr. Gorman and the sheep are out of hearing now. They must be near the shelter lot. Let's see if we can follow Tip."

"That's not so easy," Diana said. "I'm soaked through. I don't especially want to wander around in much more of this snow, anyway."

"You come with us," Trixie said. "You could *never* find your way to the house by yourself. This is fun, Di! It's not cold at all, and who cares about getting a little bit wet?"

"We've been wetter than this a thousand times, skiing and tobogganing," Honey said. "But I honestly don't see much sense in it myself, Trixie. Don't you suppose Mr. Gorman knows when he has all his sheep?"

"I suppose he does but maybe not as well as the dogs do," Trixie answered. "You just wait till Mr. Gorman gets that flock where he wants it and the gate locked. He'll know all the sheep aren't there, and he'll come back here hunting Tip to see what he's up to. I'm all for following the dog now. How about you, Brian? Jim? Mart? Honey? Di, you'll just *have* to come with us."

"I'm for it," Jim answered.

"Me, too," Honey said, close behind Brian, who patted Tip's wet head. "If we don't get going," she said, "Tip is going to wiggle right out of his skin."

"What's keeping us?" Mart called. "Wait a minute, Trix . . . Trixie, where are you?"

"Through the fence and halfway down the hill," she called back. The snow had thinned a little, and, in the beam from her flashlight, she could see the deep gully ahead. "Tip's gone crazy," she shouted. "I *know* some lost sheep must be around here someplace . . . but where?"

Slipping and sliding, the other Bob-Whites followed Trixie under the fence wires and down the slope. "There's not a thing down here!" Mart said. "Sheep couldn't get through the fence if they tried."

"Tell it to Tip!" Trixie shouted back. "I'll trust *him*. Listen to him bark!"

"Come back from that gully!" Jim shouted. "Trixie, stay away from there. Wait! It's dangerous!"

A branched dead tree had fallen across the ravine. It made a natural bridge, and Trixie started over it, following Tip.

"What's bothering you?" she called back. "It's safe enough, Jim. We *have* to get over to the other side. I'm coming, Tip. . . . Jeepers! Help! Jim! Help!"

Down she went, breaking through the branches of the dead tree . . . down . . . the collie hurtling after her. And then, just as the rest of the Bob-Whites reached

the gully's edge, Trixie's voice came up to them. "I'm
... all ... right ... but, gleeps, look what I found!"

She had landed right in the middle of a dozen or more
fat ewes. The snow, held up by the web of branches,
had formed a shed for the wandering animals. Far more
frightened by Trixie's presence than she was by her fall,
sheep baaed and bleated, tried vainly to get up the sides
of the gully, and fell back, floundering.

"Are you *sure* you aren't hurt?" Jim asked anxiously
as he and Brian let themselves cautiously down into
the slush of the creek bed.

"I'm sure of it," Trixie said. "I just had my breath
knocked out. And I'm a sight ... all covered with mud.
The poor sheep are in worse shape. What will they do?
They can't ever get out of here, Jim. They'll just die.
We'll *have* to have Mr. Gorman's help. Jim!" A sudden
thought struck Trixie. "Jim, do you suppose this could
solve the mystery of the disappearing sheep? Do you
suppose they fell in this ravine and couldn't get out?"

"Gosh, no," Jim said. "Mr. Gorman would have looked
here first thing."

"Sure," Brian said, "and the dogs would have tracked
the sheep if they wandered in here. Tip even found
them in the storm. Say, where is the storm now?"

"It's gone!" Mart said from above them.

"Even stars in the sky!" Diana exclaimed.

"Iowa weather is funnier than Westchester County
weather if that's possible," Honey said. "Mart, what
are you doing?"

57

"Trying to find my way to where Jim and Trixie and Brian are," Mart said, "and it looks as though I'll have to fall down, the way Trixie did."

"Just don't come down here at all," Trixie said. "Someone has to go and find Mr. Gorman."

"Someone has to tell us how to get out of here and how to get the sheep out," Jim added. "Mart, suppose you and the girls go back to the house and bring Mr. Gorman. Tell him where we are and what Trixie found."

"All right," Mart said, "but it's my opinion that he'd rather not see any Bob-Whites right now."

"We have given him a tough time," Jim agreed. "However, go and find him now, please."

"Do that, Mart," Trixie added, "or we'll have to start swimming. The slush down here is over my galoshes!"

"It's a real mess," Brian said. "Mart!"

Mart didn't answer. He and Diana and Honey were on their way to get help.

Trixie's Discovery • 5

BACK AT THE FARM, Mr. Gorman, with the help of Tag, had succeeded in corralling the flock where they could quickly seek shelter under the thatched sheds. He had just dropped the bar to lock the gate, when Mart appeared with the two girls.

He seemed too weary to say anything. He just whistled for Tag and started out toward the pasture again. Somewhere out there, he was sure, about twelve of his best sheep were still marooned.

"Mr. Gorman, sir!" Mart called, and he sloshed hurriedly through the snow to where the farm manager halted, waiting for him. "Mr. Gorman," he said breathlessly, "Trixie found the rest of the sheep!"

"*Trixie* found them?" Mr. Gorman repeated.

"In the gully. She fell in on top of them," Mart told him, then explained.

"The gully, of all places," Mr. Gorman said and dropped his arms with a sigh of exhaustion. "It'll be a night's work to get them out of there. Where are Brian and Jim? And where's Trixie now?"

When Mart told him they were keeping the sheep company in the ravine, he had no comment. "You'll have to help me," he said. "Go over to the house, girls, and get some dry clothing. You'll just be in the way out here," he insisted as Honey and Diana started to follow him and Mart. "My wife is worried now about all of you. I'm sure of that," he said. "Please go and tell her what's going on."

Then, as the girls obeyed him, he said to Mart, "We'll have to get a short ladder so they can climb out of that gully, and then we'll have to try and get the sheep out. It's going to take some doing."

Mart followed Mr. Gorman to the big barn, where the farm manager took a ladder from a hook on the wall and handed it to Mart, then found a shovel, a short-handled ax, and a bag of cracked corn. "Lead the way, Mart," he said, "if you have any idea where to go. It's a long gully, and the sheep could have wandered into it in half a dozen places. What a night!"

For the first time in many a day, Mart didn't have a word to say. He took up his share of the strange objects Mr. Gorman had assembled and just plodded ahead.

Back in the ravine, now that the snow had stopped, the ewes made an attempt to dry themselves. "Have a heart!" Trixie begged. "Heavens, what are you doing?" Standing well apart from one another, the ewes shook their bodies, soaking Trixie and Jim and Brian. Then, to dry their heads, they shook them so fast that nothing but a blur could be seen.

"Poor sheep!" Trixie said, trying to keep out of the way. "What a load of water their fleece holds!"

The combined shaking of heads and bodies sounded like distant thunder.

"Poor sheep," Brian imitated Trixie. "Poor us, I'd say. It's a cloudburst!"

"Mr. Gorman surely can't still be cross at us when he sees the mess we're in," Trixie said and hugged her shoulders. "Golly, but I'm cold!"

The farm manager, relieved to find both Bob-Whites and sheep safe, wasn't angry at all. "Good work, Trixie!" he said. "I was afraid for a while I'd never find the rest of the sheep in time to save them."

"Jeepers, I didn't do anything except stumble on to them," Trixie said. "Tip is the one who found them. Say, Mr. Gorman, did you ever get in the way of a sheep trying to shake itself dry?"

In spite of the strain he was under, Mr. Gorman had to laugh. "So that's what almost drowned you."

"Yes," Trixie said, trying to wring out the hem of her heavy sweater. "Mr. Gorman, we'll *never* get them out of here."

"Oh, yes, we will!" Mr. Gorman said, and he picked up the shovel and went down the ladder. "This isn't the first time this has happened, by any means. Even with the ravine fenced off, they have a way of getting through. Why, you're shaking, Trixie. Here, take my sweater. I've another under it, and I'll be warm enough when I get at this job. Give me a hand here, boys."

He handed the ax to Jim. "Go up," he said, "and chop off a few of the stoutest branches from that tree spanning the gully. Trixie, if you get through that wall of sheep, please go down a way and see if you can find a slope not quite as steep as this one."

Trixie jumped ahead to do his bidding. "Where's Tip?" she asked, suddenly aware that the dog wasn't with them.

"He got out and came back, so I shut both of them up in the barn," Mr. Gorman said. "They'd have driven us crazy, and the sheep, too. We'll follow you, Trixie, as soon as Jim cuts the branches."

Because the sheep had crowded so close to Trixie for warmth, they followed her now, like a dozen Mary's little lambs. Not far away she found a gentler slope of wall and called back to tell Mr. Gorman, who, with the boys, soon joined her.

"We'll make a sort of ramp," he said, attacking the bank with his shovel, "with shallow steps, then lay the branches on them so the sheep can get a foothold. That's right, Mart! We'll have the stairs made in no time."

Trixie watched, fascinated, and did her best to keep

the restless sheep out of the way.

"Now," Mr. Gorman said to her, "take a handful of the cracked corn out of this bag. Just let them smell it. Don't give them any right now. Sooooo—sheep! Baaa—sooooo!" he commanded. "There, Trixie, spread a little of the corn over that lower step."

Trixie did as she was told. As each step was dug out, she followed after Mr. Gorman and the boys and sprinkled some cracked corn. She watched anxiously then, as one of the ewes started to nibble timidly at the lower foothold, then struggled up to the next one. Others followed the lead sheep. Soon all were out of the gully and on solid ground.

At Mr. Gorman's bidding, the boys held up the lower fence wires, and Trixie helped the manager to herd the protesting ewes through and toward the home field.

Back home, when the sheep were safe in the sheltered fold, the weary five went into the house. Mrs. Gorman, Honey, and Diana had gone to bed, but they had left food and hot coffee.

"We're surely sorry we caused you all this trouble," Trixie said. "Maybe we can make up for it someway . . . you know . . . we just *might* be able to find some clue that will help you find the stolen sheep."

"Don't worry anymore about anything, Trixie," Mr. Gorman said, rubbing his head wearily. "It all turned out all right tonight. In the first place, I should have remembered to tell you to lock the gate. As for the stolen sheep, that's a problem for the law, not for girls and boys. I'm sorry I was so cross tonight. Mr. Belden wanted you to have fun. This business tonight can't qualify as fun, but it surely can be called adventure."

"Yes, indeed," Mart called back as the boys started through the back door for their quarters in the barn. "And adventure is Trixie's middle name, isn't it, Trix, old girl?"

Trixie didn't answer. She was halfway up the stairs. *Not a problem for boys and girls,* she said to herself. *Then why hasn't that sheriff discovered even one little tiny clue by this time? Jeepers, Honey and I have solved far bigger mysteries than this one! Not for boys and girls,* she repeated. *I'll show them!*

On the Trail • 6

TUESDAY THE SKIES were sunny. The mood of the day was reflected in the faces of everyone at the breakfast table at Happy Valley Farm. The trouble of the night before seemed to be forgotten.

"Around noon I'll let the sheep out into the pastures again," Mr. Gorman said. "There's hardly a trace of the snow left. Unfortunately, as it melts, all that water will get to the river, and sooner or later there's liable to be trouble there. Do you think you can all find something to do today?" he asked the Bob-Whites.

"We'd like to help you," Jim said. "Is there anything a bunch of amateurs can do?"

"I don't plan to do much outside of the house today,"

the manager said. "Ben will probably come back sometime this morning, and I'll run into Des Moines and pick
him up at the bus station. Maybe he'll take some of you
fishing in one of the bayous. Trixie, I don't know just
what you'll find to do. If you *have* to do some detective work, you can try and find out where Blackie has
hidden her new batch of kittens."

Trixie didn't think that last remark was funny at all.
Jim evidently didn't think so, either.

"Finding kittens shouldn't be too hard for Trixie," he
told Mr. Gorman. "You see, the sheriff of Westchester
County thinks she has some kind of second sight. She's
been responsible for the capture of some pretty tough
criminals."

"Now, now, Jim, I find that hard to believe," Mr.
Gorman said.

"It's true," Honey said loyally. "I know because I
helped her, and Trixie and I are going to have our own
detective agency when we finish college. If you'd give
her any chance at all, she could tell you who's been
taking Mr. Belden's sheep."

"Is there some kind of crystal ball she looks into?"
Mr. Gorman teased. "Go ahead, Trixie, do all the solving you want to do. Would you like to read my palm?"

"Stop teasing her," Mrs. Gorman said as she set a
plate of steaming hot pancakes on the table. "We can
be glad of any help we can get with the sheep. Sheriff
Brown doesn't seem to be getting anyplace. He's new,"
she explained to the Bob-Whites. "Tom Benton used

to be the sheriff, and he was a good one."

"Joe Brown hasn't had a chance to show what he can do," Mr. Gorman said, then changed the subject. "Satan's Baby and Black Giant could stand a run, Jim, if you and Brian want something to do. Or, if one of you has a driver's license, I'm sure Ben wouldn't mind if you were to take his old jalopy and explore the country around here. I'll get the key for you."

"I have a license," Brian said, "and so has Jim. We'll be careful."

"If you use Ben's car, don't remove the boat he has roped on top of it," Mr. Gorman said. "He keeps it there so he has it handy anytime he wants to go fishing, and he doesn't want it touched. There's an artificial lake up the road a way . . . Waterworks Park. You may want to see it. East of here a few miles, you'll find the old Army post. It's an abandoned cavalry garrison. Since you like horses so well, you may find the old stables and the parade ground interesting."

"Right now," Mrs. Gorman interrupted, "maybe you girls would like to go down to the main road after the mail. It's too nice to stay in."

"I'll go," Trixie said quickly. "There just might be a letter from Moms. Coming, Honey? Di?"

Blackie the cat ran up to them as they left the house. She rubbed her arched back against Trixie's legs. "I know," said Trixie, and she bent over to stroke the cat's back. "You want to show us your new babies. We'll look for them when we come back from the mailbox."

67

She straightened up. "And just *maybe*, later on," she said to the girls, "we'll find something much more important than little new kittens! Maybe!"

As they neared Army Post Road, Diana said, "Somebody seems to be having some trouble over there on the highway near the mailboxes. Do you think it's the postman?"

"Hardly, in a truck that size," Trixie said. "Look!" she cried and stopped halfway down the hill. "That man!"

"What man?" Honey asked.

"The one with the black beard," Trixie said. "You know—I saw him out in the field the first night we were here."

"Are you afraid of him?" Diana asked, drawing nearer to Trixie and taking her arm.

"Of course not!" Trixie said quickly. "His truck seems to be stalled. Honey Wheeler, do you see what he has in his truck?"

"Sheep," Diana said. "What about it?"

"Yes, sheep," Honey echoed. "Is *that* the man you said looked like a sheep thief, Trixie?"

"Yes," said Trixie in a low voice. "Di, you go on to the box and get the mail, will you, please? Honey and I have work to do."

"I will not," Diana said. "I wouldn't go near that truck. I'm afraid."

"Oh, all right," Trixie answered. "Go on back to the

house, then. Honey, you go back, too, and tell the boys. Try to get hold of them before they saddle the horses. I'll get the mail and then catch up with you."

When Trixie ran back down the farmhouse road, Honey and the boys were waiting. "Please take the mail into the house," she told Diana, and she thrust the package into her hand. "Brian, get Ben's jalopy. Hurry!"

Brian wheeled the car around. Trixie and Honey and Jim and Mart piled into it, and they were off up the road to the highway.

"I'm sure he's the thief," Trixie said excitedly. "I saw him that night on the hill overlooking the sheep pasture. What else could he have been doing there?"

"Are you talking to yourself?" Mart asked, looking at Trixie.

"No, I'm not, Mart Belden. I'm talking to Brian and Jim and Honey. Can't you hurry, Brian? Oh, jeepers, he must have repaired his truck," she said as they reached the intersection near Army Post Road. "He isn't even in sight."

"I'll see if I can overtake him," Brian said and stepped on the accelerator.

"There probably are speed laws," Jim reminded him. "Slow down, Brian. You're supposed to be the conservative one, you know."

"How can I slow down when Trixie's twisting my arm?" Brian asked. "She's the one who's in a hurry."

"It's all right now," Trixie said breathlessly. "There's the truck ahead, see? It's turning down that road. After it, Brian! He's making for some hideout!"

"Funny kind of hideout," Mart said. "He's heading right into Valley Park."

"Well, we're going to follow him, anyway. He's probably trying to throw us off," Trixie cried.

When the truck parked in front of the small bank, Brian drew right in beside it. Trixie was out of the jalopy in a flash. She peeked into the truck. "They're the same kind of sheep as Uncle Andrew's," she whispered. "The man's gone into the bank. I'm going to follow him. I've got to see what he does."

Inside, she went to the desk in the center of the room and pretended to be filling out a deposit slip. Out of the corner of her eye, to her surprise, Trixie saw the president of the bank come from behind his desk and shake hands with the black-bearded man.

"How are you, Mr. Schulz?" he said. "What brings you into town? Selling some more of your sheep?"

"Yes, I am," the bearded man answered. "When my neighbor, Andy Belden, was here, he kept after me to hold on to them for a better price—but I got my price at the auction at Rivervale the other day. That's where I'm bound for again."

Dejectedly Trixie trudged back to the jalopy and climbed into the front seat with Brian. She told them what she had heard. No one said a word till they left the village of Valley Park behind them.

"How was I to know?" Trixie said then, defensively. "I never met the neighbor across the road from Happy

70

Valley. Anyway, what was he doing in Uncle Andrew's field that late in the evening?"

"Part of his farm adjoins Uncle Andrew's land," Mart said. "I knew that."

"You mean his land jumps across the road?" Honey asked.

"Sure it does. When they lay out new roads, lots of times they have to cut through people's land. Mr. Gorman told us that land across the creek belonged to Mr. Schulz. I guess Trixie just wasn't listening. Dreaming, instead, about black whiskers and—"

"Cut it out, Mart," Jim said. "It *did* look suspicious."

"Even bigger brains than yours, Mart," Trixie said shamefacedly, "men like . . . well, Scotland Yard and the FBI . . . they have to track down every clue."

At the farmhouse, they found that Ben had returned. He was a big, dark, good-natured young man, anxious to talk about the short course he was planning to take at the university in Ames.

"The dean of the school of agriculture has his own big farm," Ben said. "I was out there. Mr. Gorman, you should see the queer-looking sheep he has. Wait a minute; I wrote it down. It's a kind of French merino . . . here it is . . . Rambouillet."

"You don't see many of them in Iowa," Mr. Gorman said. "As a matter of fact, I never did see one."

"They have skin as loose as a basset hound's," Ben told the Bob-Whites. "It hangs in folds. I'd hate to

71

shear one of them. The wool brings a good price, though. Maybe I'll have some of them when I get my own farm. It'd be worth a try."

"Are you going to be a sheep farmer?" Trixie asked.

"I'm going to try to be," Ben answered with a grin. "A *real* farmer with a *real* farm—not a New York farm the size of a handkerchief."

"You've been in rural New York, then?" Trixie asked, annoyed.

"No, I haven't, and I don't want to be," Ben answered. "Too much fancy stuff. Give me the wide open spaces," he sang, half under his breath.

"We have some *real* farms, as you call them, in New York," Trixie said, "and one of the best agricultural schools in the whole United States . . . Cornell."

"It's a good school," Ben conceded, "but, say, you should just get over to Iowa State before you go back home." As he got up from the table, he asked, "Did you say this outfit wanted to go fishing?"

"Yes, Ben, I think some of them would like to," Mr. Gorman said.

"Well, then, let's get going. We have to dig worms first," he added as he went out the door.

"Don't mind Ben," Mr. Gorman said. "We had a visitor from New York City last summer who patronized him till he saw red. Ben stood him just so long, then he took him snipe hunting. Don't let him catch you on that one. The poor guy held a bag open out there on the hill all night long, waiting for a snipe to go into it. Ben

72

had a good night's rest. I guess he thinks all New Yorkers are the same. He might just make an exception of your Uncle Andrew's family. He'll show you a good time fishing."

"Anybody coming?" Ben stuck his head in the door to ask. The boys jumped up to join him.

"I don't think I'll go," Trixie said.

"Are you afraid of worms?" Ben asked.

"She's not afraid of anything," Jim said. "You'll find that out. Come on with us, Trixie."

"No, thanks," Trixie said. "I have to *fry*, not *catch*." She accented her words for Ben's benefit.

"Doesn't he think he's smart?" she asked Honey and Diana when they were all doing the luncheon dishes for Mrs. Gorman. "I think there's something just a little bit odd about him."

"Do you think he's a sheep thief?" Honey asked, laughing. "He doesn't have a black beard, you know."

"Black beard?" Mrs. Gorman asked.

"Yes—" Honey began.

"Honey Wheeler," Trixie said under her breath, "Honey Wheeler, if you say one word to anyone about that . . . well, you can just forget all about our plans for an agency when we finish school. I'm going upstairs and write a letter to Moms."

A Strange Light · 7

ABOUT SIX O'CLOCK, the fishermen returned with four good-sized bass and about a dozen bluegills. The boys cleaned them, and then, under Mrs. Gorman's direction, Trixie rolled the fish in cornmeal and browned them in butter.

Ben came in and ruffled Trixie's curls. "You aren't mad at me, are you?" he asked. "I always have liked to tease people. The boys were telling me about some of the bad *hombres* you've hunted down. I take off my hat to you."

Trixie turned the crisp fish onto a warmed platter, then led Ben to a box in the corner of the kitchen.

"Hunting these down was the most fun I ever had,"

she said, and she picked up a little black and white kitten and held it to her cheek. "Isn't it darling?"

"Well, I'll be darned," Ben said. "I've hunted all over for Blackie's kittens. I'll bet she really had them hidden. Where did you find them?"

"In the closet in your room where you keep your summer clothes," Trixie said triumphantly. "You must have left the door to your closet open. Mrs. Gorman asked me to bring the towels out of your room—she's going to wash clothes tomorrow—and I noticed the open closet door. I started to close it, and there they were—four of them." Trixie sat on the floor and pulled the kittens into her lap.

"Right in my own room!" Ben said, chagrined. "Almost under my own nose!"

"No, right on top of your good summer sport coat," Trixie answered. "They think it's a nice soft bed, don't you, kittens?"

"Well, I'll be doggoned," Ben said as he held a little black kitten in his hand. "Listen to this little fellow purr, will you? Sounds like a motorboat. There, there," he told the little cat, "I can get that old summer coat cleaned. Don't be so scared. Its heart is going about a hundred and sixty beats to the second," he said, and he put the tiny ball of fur into Trixie's hands. "They sure are cute."

Afterward, when they stood around the piano singing while Diana played, Trixie whispered to Honey, "At first I thought I wasn't going to like Ben at all, but he's really

75

nice, isn't he? I guess I like him, after all."

A few hours later, something happened to send Trixie's thoughts hurrying back to her first impression of Ben.

About eleven-thirty, after they had all gone to bed, Trixie still lay awake. The house was quiet. It was quiet outside. Tip and Tag were asleep or off about their dog business in the far fields. Betsy and her calf were quiet. There was no moon, but the stars were so thick in the great bowl of sky that they shed a sort of half-light.

Suddenly, out of the quiet, Trixie heard two soft whistled notes, one high, one low. Then, after an interval, two more notes.

Mart's signal! she thought. *Our emergency signal! What can it be?*

Trixie slid out of bed, put on her jeans, and drew a sweater over her head. She slipped her feet into sneakers and went quietly down the stairs and through the door.

"It's Ben!" Mart said. "He pretended to go to bed when we did, but I don't think he ever did."

"What happened?" Trixie whispered.

"He just left here with a lantern," Mart answered. "See that light bobbing up the road? He's trying to shade it with his hand—see, Trixie—right over there past Schulz's barn?"

"I see," said Trixie. "That's funny, isn't it? Where do you think he's going? That's a silly question. You don't know any more than I do. Mart, let's follow him! Let's see what he's doing. Do you have your flashlight?"

In answer, Mart turned the light on and flashed it up and down the road.

"Don't do that!" Trixie exclaimed softly. "He'll find out we're following him. Just turn it down on the road so we can see. Let's run!"

They ran as fast as they could, keeping the bobbing light of Ben's lantern in sight. Across Army Post Road he went, down Sand Hill, and along the trail that led to Walnut Woods.

Trixie and Mart followed. Just inside the entrance to the woods, they lost sight of Ben. "I *thought* when we passed this woods coming from the airport that it looked like a criminal's hideout," Trixie said.

Mart didn't answer. "There goes his lantern again, Trix," he said excitedly. "He's making some sort of signal with it."

"He is," Trixie agreed, her voice tense. "He's swinging it around in an arc. Look, Mart! Look way beyond him, back there farther in the woods. Do you see anything?"

"A square of light," Mart said. "Can it be a window?"

"Probably," Trixie said. "If it is, someone just drew the curtain down. Mart, this doesn't look at all good to me. There goes Ben's lantern again, signaling."

"Yes," Mart said, "it's some kind of rendezvous. Let's get going, Trixie."

"All right," Trixie said and started toward the woods.

Mart caught her hand, drew her back, and shook his head. "Huh-uh," he said, "not in there. We don't know our way six feet ahead of us. Getting lost in Walnut Woods wouldn't do us any good in solving the mystery."

"Well, Mart Belden, of all the crazy things! If you think I'm going to stop now—"

"Not stop," Mart answered. "Just be smart for once in your life, Trixie. Let's go back to the house as quickly as we can, tell Mr. Gorman what's going on, and then come back here with him. He knows the woods."

Reluctantly Trixie turned and ran—ran up Sand Hill, across Army Post Road, down the farmhouse road, and into Happy Valley Farm. Breathlessly she knocked at Mr. Gorman's door, Mart close behind her.

When he opened the door, Mrs. Gorman came out, too. Honey and Diana, aroused, poked their heads from their doors down the hall.

"It's Ben!" Trixie gasped.

"What about Ben? Is he sick?" Mr. Gorman asked.

"He's the thief!" Trixie gasped. "Mart and I caught him red-handed!"

"You what?" Mr. Gorman demanded. "Ben a thief? What rank nonsense! What are you talking about?"

Dramatically Trixie told him, with Mart trying to talk at the same time.

When Mr. Gorman could piece together what they were saying sufficiently to understand them, he laughed. He laughed, and he laughed. And then Mrs. Gorman laughed, too, till she almost cried.

Trixie and Mart just stood there getting angrier and angrier. Finally, Trixie stamped her foot on the floor and said, "Stop that! Don't you *want* to find out what is happening to the sheep?"

"We sure do, Trixie," Mr. Gorman said. "Sure as you're born. Only Ben isn't stealing the sheep."

"How do you know," Trixie asked, "when you won't even go and find out? What else could he be doing, sneaking off into the night that way and swinging his lantern around, signaling?"

"Hunting possums," Mrs. Gorman said and put her arm around Trixie. "If there's anything in the world Ben likes, it's roast possum. On dark nights he goes after them . . . trees them and blinds them with his lantern. Wait till tomorrow when you taste the fat one he brings home."

"I don't want to taste one. I'd never in the world taste one," Trixie said. "I'd just as soon eat . . . Blackie or Tip or Tag!"

"Whew!" Mr. Gorman said. "You should have the red hair instead of Jim. Sheep thief!" Mr. Gorman was still laughing as he turned back into his room. "Wait till I tell this to Ben! Trixie, remember what I said about leaving the problem to Joe Brown, the sheriff? That remark still stands. Get some sleep now, girls. You, too, Mart. Ben a sheep thief! Imagine that, Mary!"

Trixie didn't move. "Maybe we *did* make a mistake," she said. "Maybe Ben isn't a sheep thief. Maybe it's true that he was swinging the lantern to blind the possum. But what about that lighted window off in the woods? And why did someone pull down the blind when Ben swung his lantern?"

"Yes, sir," Mart repeated, "how about that?"

"Imagination," Mr. Gorman said. "There's no house off in that woods. Imagination—just imagination."

Bob-Whites in the Spotlight • 8

LISTEN TO THIS." Trixie spread the letter from her mother on the table in the breakfast nook. "Listen, Jim —all of you! Moms said that Dan stopped in to see her and get news of us, and guess what!"

"I'll see for myself," Mart said, taking their mother's letter. "Gosh . . . old Dan has himself a job!"

"How can he?" Honey asked. "He couldn't come with us because he had to be tutored this vacation. What kind of a job?"

"After he gets through with his lessons," Mart said. "It's a honey of a job. I wish I had a chance at it. He's giving figure skating lessons part time at the White Plains rink."

"That's perfect for Dan!" Diana said.

"Something else Moms said," Trixie announced. "Dan told her we should have taken our skates with us, so she sent them. They'll probably get here after we leave. I wonder what Dan thought we'd do with skates out here in the country?"

"There's a good indoor rink at Rivervale," Ben remarked as he stopped in the kitchen for a second cup of coffee. "And *our* rink is open day and night. Happy Valley isn't exactly the last frontier."

"We know that," Honey said quickly. "Don't be so edgy, Ben. We think it's swell here. When our skates come, we'll try out the rink. That is, if you'll lend us your jalopy to get over there."

"I think I can manage that," Ben said. "Say, Trixie," he went on, winking at Jim, "when are you going to slip the handcuffs on me?"

"You told!" Trixie accused Mr. Gorman.

"Of course I did," Mr. Gorman said. "If Ben is stealing my sheep, I want him to stop it right now."

"Well, I just think it was mean of you to tell him," Trixie said, her face bright red.

"Can't you tell when they're teasing you?" Mrs. Gorman asked. "I think it's real good of you to try to find out who's stealing those sheep, Trixie. I know one thing—if someone doesn't find out pretty soon, most of our ewes will be gone, and then—"

"It won't be long till I'm gone, too . . . no longer manager of Happy Valley Farm. That's what you mean, isn't it, Mary?" Mr. Gorman's face was serious.

Ben's face sobered, too. "That's right," he said. "One thing you said sort of stays in my mind, Trixie. About that lighted window you thought you saw off in the woods . . . back of the place where I was treeing the possum."

"Yes?" Trixie asked, immediately alert. "We did see it, and we saw someone pull the shade down, didn't we, Mart?"

"It couldn't be," Ben said, shaking his head. "I hunt in the woods all the time, and I fish in the river at this end of the woods. Been doing it for years. Nobody has ever cut through the grapevines and hazel brush to get very far back in that jungle. The ground belongs to the state, you know. It's really Walnut *State* Park."

"We have heard stories about people living back in there," Mrs. Gorman reminded him.

"They did about a hundred years ago, yes," Ben agreed. "You see, Trixie, the way I heard it is this: Just after the Civil War ended, a bunch of men, led by some escaped convicts, gathered their families together and settled along the banks of the river. They made their living by operating illicit stills."

"Then the government caught up with them," Mrs. Gorman said.

"Yes." Ben nodded. "And no one knows quite what happened. I have heard that they went farther back into the deep woods. Even if they did, no one has seen anything of them or their descendants since that time."

83

"People have seen lights in there before," Mrs. Gorman reminded him.

"It was nothing but will-o'-the-wisps over the swampy land," Mr. Gorman said. "Say, I almost forgot something." He reached into his shirt pocket and drew out a handful of tickets. "Dan Schulz's boy, Ned, sold me these. There's a basketball game at Rivervale this afternoon, with a barbecue and dance afterward. I thought you might all like to go."

"We'd love it," Trixie said, and she forgot all about Walnut Woods for the moment.

"It's to raise money for their school. It starts around two o'clock, I think. Rivervale High has a pretty good team," Mr. Gorman said. "Ned plays center. He's been wanting to meet Jim and Brian and Mart . . . you girls, too, I'm sure."

"I'm not so sure about the girls," Mrs. Gorman said as she put away the breakfast dishes the girls had finished washing and drying. "Ned never seems to have much on his mind but hunting and basketball and football . . . skating, too, I believe."

"He's what the girls would have called a 'sheik' when I was your age," Mr. Gorman teased. "Tall, dark, and handsome."

"Let's just hope he can play basketball," Jim said. "Say, Mr. Gorman, it sure was swell of you to get us those tickets."

"Don't mention it," Mr. Gorman answered. "We won't need the station wagon today, and if you think you can manage it and find your way to Rivervale, you may use it."

"Thanks a lot," Trixie said. "Ben, won't you come along with us?"

"Too much studying to do," Ben answered. "But thanks!"

The Bob-Whites gave the horses a quick run round the farm, up the road to Waterworks Park, and back. Then, after a light lunch, they piled into the station wagon and were off.

The girls wore sweaters and skirts, for Mrs. Gorman said it was all quite informal, and the dance would be in the gym. In view of what was to happen later on, it was just as well that Trixie, at least, didn't dress up.

The Bob-Whites found seats right down in front, near the center of the court. A dozen or so Rivervale High players, with huge *R*'s on their jackets, were warming up.

It wasn't hard to tell which of the players was Ned Schulz. He was the tallest, the darkest, and the handsomest. Automatically Honey smoothed back her long hair, and Diana batted her curly lashes for a better look at him.

Trixie, though, followed Ned's quick, perfectly timed progress around the floor, and, as the ball left his hands, arched into the air, and ripped through the basket, she whistled in quick admiration.

Ned heard her and, realizing that these were his

neighbor's out-of-town visitors, came up to introduce himself.

"We're waiting for the gang from Indianola High," he said. "Something must have held them up."

"It's been fun watching the warm-up," Trixie said enthusiastically. "You have some neat players."

"Thanks. Do any of you play for your school back home?" Ned asked. "Where is it, now, someplace in New York?"

"Sleepyside Junior-Senior High," Trixie said. "Jim and Brian and Mart all play."

"Do you girls play, too?" Ned asked. "Say, wait a minute till I see what the coach is saying to the rest of the gang."

"There'll be a half or three-quarters of an hour delay," he told the Bob-Whites when he came back. "How about throwing the ball around a little?" he asked Brian and Jim and Mart. "Coach said the team should take it easy, so the floor is free. Plenty of sneakers over here under the bench."

"That'll be keen," Mart said.

The Rivervale players sat around on the floor and on the bench while the boys from Sleepyside found sneakers to fit.

"Lace 'em up tight," one of the local players said and smiled at the boy sitting next to him.

"Yeah, thanks," Mart answered, looking up sideways at him. "I seem to remember that."

"No harm meant," the boy replied. "I just thought

maybe you hadn't played much."

"He'll be sorry he ever said that," Honey whispered to Trixie. "This is going to be fun."

Mart was out on the floor in a flash. Skillfully he faked, eluded an imaginary player, reversed, faked again, and flipped the ball accurately into the basket.

Brian caught it on the bounce, pounded it to get the feel of it in his hand, dribbled it across the court, and sank a ripper from far out.

By this time the spectators on the benches were aware that the strangers on the floor were no strangers to the game of basketball. They whistled and clapped and stamped their feet.

Mart stopped practice-shooting at the far end of the court, bent, clowning, and bowed elaborately. This set everyone laughing. Suddenly they were quiet again, for Jim started to move slowly clockwise around the board, stopping only long enough at each position to aim, flick his wrist, and send the ball through the basket, never missing.

Then, oblivious to the crowd, all three boys were out on the floor. Jim sent the ball flying to Brian, who was less than a dozen feet from the basket, then raced forward to recover it if Brian missed it. He did miss; Jim recovered and, almost directly under the basket, sent the ball through. Picking it up, he then hurled a long pass back to Mart, who leaped, caught the ball, and, with a quick one-handed shot, sent it against the backboard and through the basket.

As the crowd cheered and cheered, the boys, looking embarrassed, ran back to the bench where the girls were waiting with Ned Schulz.

"Good going!" Ned said and shook hands with the three Bob-Whites.

"We were just hamming it up," Brian apologized.

"They—our team, I mean—were district champions in Westchester County," Trixie said proudly as she took a ball from Mart and walked up and down in front of the group, pounding it on the floor.

"I can believe that, all right," Ned said. "Say, Trixie, how about you? That ball is used for something besides bouncing. Come on, throw it out!"

"Sink one and show him!" Jim said under his breath to Trixie.

She shook her head. "Not in front of all this crowd." Then, stung by a snickering laugh from the same boy who had taunted Mart, she forgot where she was, stood up, sighted the basket, took her stance, and sent the ball high in the air and straight through the basket.

"Hey, do that again!" Ned called, and he tossed the ball back to her.

It wasn't too hard for Trixie, who had spent hours practicing spot shots at the hoop on the garage at Crabapple Farm. She caught the ball and, without changing her position on the sideline, not far from midcourt, sent it flying back again, then again and again. Every time it soared neatly through the basket.

Amid catcalls and cheering, she sat down beside Jim.

"I couldn't do that again in a million years," she said.

The Rivervale coach had been sitting watching the Bob-Whites perform and scribbling on the clipboard on his knee. As the players from Indianola High finally appeared and went through the gym, he rose to follow them, then stopped to speak to the Bob-Whites. In response to his questions, they told him their names and the name of their school.

"Pretty good ball," he said and shook hands with the boys. "And Trixie," he turned to her and said, "I could use an accurate shooter like you on the team today."

He didn't need one. Rivervale High played a brilliant game. The score was Rivervale seventy-six, Indianola forty-two.

After the game, the Bob-Whites, who were unanimous in wishing they hadn't been such limelighters, found themselves surrounded by a cordial, friendly crowd of Rivervale fans.

Boys milled around Honey and Diana, trying to get their attention and book them for dances later. Trixie, hair tousled and face flushed, stayed close to Brian and Mart and Jim. As one of the Rivervale fans slapped her on the back, with a quick word of praise for her basket shots, she sent a wistful glance toward Diana and Honey. They both looked so pretty and appealing.

Sometimes, she said to herself, *I wish I could remember to be a girl instead of a tomboy. Especially when there'll be dancing.*

Two Suspects • 9

AFTER THE GAME, the girls went into the school rest room to wash their hands and freshen their lipstick.

"That Ned Schulz has everything, hasn't he, Trixie?" Honey asked as she ran her comb through her shoulder-length brown hair. "And you used a pretty sneaky way to get him interested in you."

"Yes, wasn't I a show-off?" Trixie answered. "I was, wasn't I, Honey? I honestly forgot where I was. When that boy challenged me, I just had to prove that I could hit the basket. Was it too awful?"

"If you were anyone else, I'd have been sure you were doing it to attract Ned," Honey assured her. "The last thing in the world you'd ever be is a show-off."

It worried Trixie, though. "Do you think anyone else thought I was trying to attract Ned's attention?" she asked.

"Only about fifty percent of the girls in the gym," Diana said. "Never mind, Trix. It was sensational. They don't know your heart belongs to Jim."

"I like Jim, of course," Trixie said, blushing, "just the way you like Mart and Honey likes Brian. My heart doesn't belong to anyone."

"I know that," Diana said. "I was only teasing."

"We're all too young," Honey said. "At least, people keep telling us so."

"*My* mother and *my* daddy have known one another since they were ten years old," Diana said. "And Mother told me that she knew, even then, that she was going to marry Daddy someday."

"It does happen, I guess," Honey said.

Trixie didn't say anything, but it took her longer than usual to brush her sandy curls, and she borrowed some of Diana's spray perfume.

"Mmmm, you smell like a flower shop," Jim told her when the boys met the girls outside of the gym.

"Is it too much?" Trixie asked nervously. "It's Di's. I was sort of warm after that crazy basket-throwing. I wish I hadn't done that."

"Well, why not?" Jim asked. "You were a wow! They were baiting you, anyway, Trixie. You just *had* to sink those shots. Forget it, will you?" He pressed her arm and looked down at her, reassuring her. Suddenly

91

Trixie was comfortable again and not worried about anything.

When the Bob-Whites went into the gym, where tables were now set up and spread for the barbecue, Trixie was immediately surrounded by boys, most of them players from the Rivervale and Indianola teams. They were all talking at once . . . basketball talk.

When Trixie looked around, she discovered that Honey had gone off with a group of boys, that Diana was in a corner of the gym surrounded by another half dozen, and that Jim and Brian and Mart were in the midst of a crowd of some of the prettiest girls she had ever seen.

As Trixie watched, a tall blond girl—prettier, almost, than Diana or Honey—took hold of Jim's arm, led him to a place at the long table, and then sat down beside him. When other girls came up to talk to Jim, the tall blonde gestured to them to stay away, laughing as she did it and pointing to herself, as much as to say, "He's mine. Hands off!"

"She's as old as Jim, probably a senior, and, gosh, she's beautiful!" Trixie said, half to herself. Then suddenly she was aware that Ned had taken her arm and was leading her to a place at the table.

"Did you say something?" he asked.

Trixie shook her head. "No," she said, "but I was thinking how good everything smells. I'm hungry. Where are they cooking that meat? What kind is it?"

"Lamb," Ned answered. "An uncle of one of our guys has a restaurant near the airport. He sent his cook over to barbecue the lamb. He sent a couple of portable electric spits, too. They're big enough for a whole lamb. The meat roasts as it turns."

"I don't think I ever tasted barbecued lamb," Trixie said. "Mmmm . . . does it smell good!"

"The chef was rubbing it with some garlic," Ned said, "and it smelled horrible then. Right now it doesn't seem like the same stuff. We were going to have barbecued spareribs," Ned went on, "but a couple of men showed up with fresh lamb carcasses and offered to sell them real cheap. The committee decided to have them instead. We'll save money that way."

A light as bright as an electric bulb began to burn in Trixie's brain.

"Who were the men?" she asked.

"I don't know," Ned said. "I talked to one of them. He said they had a frozen-food locker in Valley Park. These carcasses hadn't been frozen, but if we didn't take them, they'd have to go into the locker, and it was already pretty full. He offered them real cheap, and, well, we're trying to make money on the barbecue."

"Didn't anyone on the committee think there was anything queer about such an arrangement?"

"Well, no. I guess some of them knew all about the locker. Why are you so bothered? Do you think you're going to get poisoned?"

"No," Trixie said seriously, "I'm not worried about

93

that. It just sounded too much like coincidence. There they were with the lambs, freshly killed, and here you were with a barbecue coming up."

"Say, you think of a lot of things that other girls don't," Ned said. Trixie wasn't sure whether he meant that as a compliment.

At the other side of the table, Jim was laughing and teasing the tall blond girl. Defiantly Trixie turned to Ned with a bewitching smile. She had watched Diana use such a smile to good advantage many times. "How do you know what girls think about?" she asked. "I'll bet you just imagine all sorts of things. What do you think I'm thinking right now, for instance?"

"I don't know," Ned said, "but all at once you sure don't act natural. That's what's the matter with girls. They don't act natural. I thought you were different."

"That's what boys always say," Trixie answered as she saw Jim put his arm across the chair back of the tall blond girl and lean over to talk to her. "And when girls act natural, boys lose interest."

"Not me," Ned said. "I don't go in much for girls, anyway. I don't have much time."

"I guess you wouldn't," Trixie said, "if you play basketball."

"And baseball and football. I like all sports, and we have the best coach in the whole country."

"I'd match our Sleepyside coach against him any time," Trixie said loyally.

"Well, maybe," Ned admitted. "He must be an ace

basketball coach, anyway. Anyone could tell that from the way you and Jim and Brian and Mart threw that ball around. Say, I saw you go by on Mr. Belden's Satan's Baby this morning, coming back from Waterworks Park. You sure know how to ride! I don't know why all girls aren't interested in sports." Ned motioned down the table to where Honey and Diana and some of the girls of Rivervale High were laughing and teasing the boys. "Don't they act crazy?" he asked. "All they think about is dancing and lipsticks and combing their hair. Phooey!"

"You couldn't be more mistaken," Trixie said. "Honey and Di can both shoot a basketball better than I can. They can ride better than I can. They can swim better than almost anyone and skate better, too. I just happened to be the one who got into the limelight!"

"Gee whiz, I didn't say anything about Honey or Di," Ned said hastily. "You act as though you'd like to haul off and hit me. They may be able to ride and all that, but just look at them right now . . . both using lipsticks!"

"I think I may need to use mine," Trixie said and took out her compact.

Ned laughed. "You're just doing that because you're irritated with me. They're clearing the floor now for dancing. There's some sense to dancing. It's exercise."

He's just about the queerest boy I ever met, Trixie thought to herself. *I just have to get Jim and tell him about those lamb carcasses. I know whoever sold them*

95

*to the school has something to do with Uncle Andrew's
stolen sheep.*

"You *are* sore at me," Ned said. "You haven't said
a word."

"I'm not sore about anything. I was just thinking
about something. Ned?"

"Yes?"

"If I tell you something, will you promise not to say
anything about it to anyone?"

"Sure. What is it?"

"Well, it's just this: I think those lambs that your
school committee bought at such a bargain were stolen
lambs. And I think they were stolen from my Uncle
Andrew."

Whee-ew! Ned whistled. "What makes you think
that? The men said they had a locker in Valley Park."

"You don't *know* they have one, do you?" Trixie
lowered her voice. "Someone has been stealing my
uncle's sheep and lambs regularly. He's been terribly
worried about it, and so have Mr. and Mrs. Gorman.
I'm going to find out who's been doing the stealing."

"*You're* going to find out?" Ned asked, amazed. "Now
I've heard everything. I remember my dad saying
someone had been stealing Mr. Belden's sheep. That's
why we put ours in the barns every night. But then,
we have that extra barn down near the river and
have plenty of room. I guess the sheriff is the one who'll
find out who the thieves are."

"It's been going on for a long time, and he hasn't

turned up one clue. I've only been working on the case for a few days, and now I've turned up a real hot clue. Don't you say one word to anyone, Ned Schulz. Don't forget, you promised."

"Sure I promised. I won't say anything, at least for now. But, holy cow, a girl detective!"

"Honey and I are both detectives. At least, we're going to be really, truly ones when we're older. We've solved some pretty mysterious cases at home . . . some the sheriff couldn't solve."

"Are you kidding me, Trixie?" Ned asked. "A pretty girl like you a detective?"

"I'm telling you the truth. I'll prove it to you before we go back home, or my name isn't Trixie Belden. Ned, don't you know anything more about those men who sold you the lambs?"

"Not a thing except what I've told you."

"Would you know them if you saw them again?"

"I think so. Why?"

"If you even think you see someone who looks like them, tell me, will you?"

"Sure I will. Look, Trixie, everyone's left the table but you and me. They want to take this table away so we can dance. Dance with me, will you?"

"I'd love to, Ned." Trixie smoothed back her curls and smiled at him. *He did say 'a pretty girl like you,'* she thought. *People are always saying Honey and Di are pretty. Imagine me pretty, with my mousy hair and freckles!* Sadly her eyes followed the blond girl and Jim.

Aloud she said, "That sounds like a neat orchestra."

"It's a bunch of Drake University students from Des Moines," Ned said. "Boy, can they make music!" He put his arm around Trixie's waist and whirled her out onto the floor.

On the other side of the room, Jim and the blond girl were dancing. They seemed unaware of anyone else on the floor, so animated was their conversation. A strange feeling Trixie had never known before stole over her. Could it be? Yes, it was—jealousy.

Furious with herself and furious with Jim, she threw back her head to laugh gaily at something Ned was saying . . . something he was saying that she didn't even hear. *I just don't care if I ever speak to Jim again in my life*, she thought.

Then the music slowed. Jim and the blond girl danced across the room. They stopped suddenly, just in front of Trixie and Ned.

"*Some* band!" Jim said, and he introduced the tall blond girl to Trixie. "Best barbecue I ever tasted in my life," he told Ned.

The blond girl, Dot, was beautiful. *No wonder Jim thinks she's wonderful. No wonder he can't seem to see anyone else*, Trixie thought.

"Next dance, Trix?" Jim asked as the music started up and couples moved onto the floor.

"Yes, Jim," Trixie said, and she put her hand in his and was happy.

"It's you and me, then, Dot," Ned said.

Trixie Gets Teased · 10

AS THE HOUR grew late, Trixie danced again with Jim. "It isn't the same here as it is at our dances at home," she said. "I must have danced with a dozen different boys instead of just one."

"Yes, I noticed you were having quite a ball. Are you really having a good time? Ned Schulz seems to have the Indian sign on you."

"And Dot seems to have the Indian sign on you. You've been her slave all evening!"

"Why, Trixie." Jim stopped dancing right in the middle of the floor and led Trixie to a bench at the side of the room. "You're fooling!" he said.

"I'm not! If you like that glamour type best, you're

just welcome to her. I mean it!"

"I like both kinds," Jim said. "Dot *is* glamorous. She's really glamorous. She went out of her way to be nice to me, and I appreciate it."

"I can see that you do," Trixie said. Then she added wistfully, "Oh, Jim, I wish I'd been born beautiful!"

"The *other* kind of girl," Jim went on, "didn't dress up just to impress me or any other boy. She never does. She's genuine and so comfortable to be around. She's my choice of the two. Right now her sandy curls need combing, and she sure could use some lipstick!"

Trixie's heart did a backflip. She reached frantically for her lipstick, then gave up and smiled. "That was sweet," she said. "I've been catty, and all the time I secretly thought Dot was super. Say, Jim, what I want to find out, and soon, is who those men are who sold the committee the lambs for tonight. I think they may be the thieves. Ned told me he'd let me know right away if he ever saw them again."

"That's a big help."

"It isn't much, is it? But right now, it's the only lead I have. I've hardly had a chance to talk to Honey about it. And the others don't even know I have a clue."

"We'll have to huddle on it when we get back to Happy Valley Farm and then plan the next move," Jim said. "Trixie, I think the dance is beginning to break up. The music has a slow beat. Is it getting late?"

"Probably midnight or near it," Trixie said. "Ned told me they have to stop dancing then. It's a school rule that's strictly enforced at Rivervale High."

"He told me that everybody gangs up at an all-night diner up the street. He wanted us to meet him there. Shall we?" Jim asked.

"Let's do," Trixie said enthusiastically. "Maybe I can learn something more about those men."

The music stopped. The orchestra put away their instruments. Brian, Honey, Mart, and Diana found their coats and located Jim and Trixie.

"I've something exciting to tell you!" Trixie whispered. "Wait till we get in the station wagon. Oh, there's Ned, and he's alone. Maybe he wants to ride back with us. Ned . . . Ned!"

Ned came toward them swinging his coat over his arm.

"Do you have any room for me?" he asked. "Dad dropped me off early this afternoon. I told him I'd bum a ride back with someone. Are you sure there's room?"

"Loads of it," Honey and Diana chorused.

"Do you want to stop at the diner?" Ned asked. "It'll be a madhouse. Everyone tries to get waited on at once."

"I'm not a bit hungry," Trixie said.

"I'm not, either," Honey said, "but we did promise to stop there, didn't we, Di? Say, Trixie, what's the exciting thing you were going to tell us?"

Quickly she briefed them on what she had learned from Ned.

"Trixie Belden!" Honey said, so excited she grabbed

101

Brian's arm and almost sent the wagon into a ditch. "Trixie Belden, I never saw anything like the way you manage to hunt things out! What next?"

"Wait for the next move they make, it seems to me," Jim said.

"Go and eat," Mart said. "We sure can't go hunting those men at midnight. I'm hungry, if nobody else is. That girl I sat next to at the table talked such a blue streak it kept me busy answering her. And then all I could say was 'yes,' 'uh-huh,' 'no.' "

"That was Pam Watson," Ned said, grinning. "She's a nonstop talker. Yakety-yakety-yak."

"She's cute, anyway," Mart said. "And she can dance like nobody's business. Did you see us?"

"Who could miss it?" Diana asked. She'd had such a wonderful time dancing that she hadn't seemed to notice what Mart was doing. Now, however, she had to tease him a little.

I can learn a lot about how to act with boys just by watching Di, Trixie thought. *It comes naturally to her, though.* Aloud she said, "Well, let's go in. What's the matter with you, Ned? What are you sputtering about?"

"That—that—that truck!" Ned managed to say. "That one just pulling out—over there, Brian—those are the two men who sold us the lambs. Watch out. Duck in here, back of the bus from Indianola High. There, they've pulled out now."

"After them!" Trixie commanded Brian.

"Give them a chance to get started," Ned warned.

"Don't let them know we're following them! Now, Brian, they've turned off toward the Raccoon River. Slow—but let's be sure to keep them in sight!"

"Are you *sure* they're the same men?" Trixie asked.

"I couldn't be more sure," Ned said. "The one in that heavy lumber jacket—he's the one we talked to. Say, if that wasn't a lucky break!"

"It was," Trixie agreed. "Don't lose them, Brian. Can't you go a little faster?"

"He can," Jim answered, "and then they'll know they're being followed. Calm down, Trixie!"

He might have saved his breath, because Trixie, who sat with Jim, just behind Brian, kept bobbing up and down in the seat. "Is that their taillight?" she asked. "There are two trucks ahead of us. Darn it, we've lost them. No, there they are again, or is that the truck we're trying to follow? Is that Army Post Road we're coming to?"

"That's what it is," Ned answered, "and they're the same two men, I'm sure. They've crossed Army Post Road. They're down Sand Hill. They're getting near the river and the woods."

"They're turning onto the woods road!" Trixie called. "Follow them, Brian!"

"What do you think I'm doing?" he asked. "We'll be lucky if we don't land in the river ourselves. Ned won't even let me drive with the lights on."

"It would be a dead giveaway that someone is after them," Mart said. "Gosh, Brian, I'd better turn

103

my flashlight down on the road so you can see the shoulder."

"Somebody do some thing," Diana called. "We'll all be drowned in the river. I wish you'd dropped me off at Happy Valley Farm."

"Don't be a baby," Trixie said. "Go faster, Brian. I can't even see them now."

"I'm scared," Diana said, "and I don't care who knows it. I don't want to be a detective, and I don't even want to be a detective's assistant."

"We're all right," Honey assured her. "Brian can see the road now, with Mart's flashlight. We don't seem to be getting anyplace, though."

"We are, too, Honey Wheeler!" Trixie shouted. "There, off in the woods . . . see?"

"See what?" Jim asked.

"That light flickering," Trixie said. "It's the same light I saw the night we followed Ben. I just know there's a cabin or something back there."

"It could be the will-o'-the-wisp that Mr. Gorman mentioned," Diana said. "And I think that's what you're chasing, Trixie."

"I can see a light," Jim said. "Way back. Boy, is it dark around here! The light's gone now, Trixie."

"Just as though someone pulled a shade," Trixie said. "What's the matter, Brian? Why are you stopping?"

"Because there isn't any more road, that's why," Brian said. "And I don't know what we're after, anyway. I haven't seen a taillight since we turned off that other road. I wonder where we are."

"We sure are at the end of the road," Ned said. "I've never been this far into this side of the woods. We've only lived here a year. Anybody would have to have a machete to cut through this jungle. How can we turn around, Brian?"

"We can't," Brian said and cut off the engine.

"Are we just going to sit here all night?" Diana asked. "Oh, dear, what was that noise?"

"A bullfrog." Ned laughed. "A wild, ferocious bullfrog, Di. I'll get out and have a look at the situation. Come on, fellas."

"Jeepers, but I hate to give up now," Trixie said. "I *know* those men are the thieves. How could they disappear into thin air? They had to go someplace."

"You can search me," Brian answered. "I'm interested right now in getting out of here."

"If you want to pursue the search farther, my dear intrepid sibling," Mart said, "you go off on foot—unaccompanied."

"You'd never let her do that, would you?" Diana asked. "I won't stir an inch if you do."

"Forget it, Di," Brian said. "You should know Mart by this time. Say, I think I can back out of here all right if you go ahead and train your flashlights down on the road. If those men *are* back in there someplace, I'd just as soon stay out of their way. They may be armed."

The four flashlights, two on each side of the road, furnished enough light so that Brian could back the car until he reached the point where the road had entered the woods. There he turned on the car lights and headed the car toward Happy Valley Farm.

"I've heard all kinds of stories about those old woods —people getting lost and all that. I never believed them before, but I do now," Ned said. "It sure is a mystery what happened to that truck."

"I don't think they took the same road we did at all," Jim said. "I mean when they got right up to the woods. I'd like to come down here and take a look in the daytime."

"Why don't we just get out and go back with our flashlights and see what we can find?" Trixie suggested.

"That, Beatrix Belden," Mart said, "is the wildest idea you ever had in your life, and you've had some wild ones."

How Trixie hated that name "Beatrix," and now Mart had to say it—in front of Ned, too!

"I'll settle that question," Brian said. "This bus doesn't make any more stops till it gets to Happy Valley Farm. So stop bickering."

Back at the farmhouse, the Bob-Whites all insisted on Ned's coming into the house with them for something to eat. "Gosh, yes," Mart said, "come on in, Ned. I hope there's something to eat. Mrs. Gorman probably left something out."

She had—a Thermos of hot chocolate, bags of potato chips, a jar of peanut butter, and a loaf of bread, with a bottle opener nearby to remind them of colas in the refrigerator.

"Where do you suppose Tip and Tag are?" Jim wondered. "I thought they'd be in the house, when they didn't come up the road to meet us."

"That's right, isn't it?" Trixie said, and she explained to Ned. "Mr. Gorman told us he never lets the dogs out till everyone is in the house."

"They just might flush out the thieves if he did leave them out all evening," Mart said, "but then, he knows how to run a sheep farm better than we do."

"I hear the dogs barking now," Trixie said and peered out the window. "It must be Mr. Gorman just coming from the barn. I can see his lantern."

She opened the door, and the dogs came rushing ahead of Mr. Gorman and into the house, jumping up on all of them.

"Down, Tip!" Trixie commanded. "Is anything wrong, Mr. Gorman?"

"Not yet," Mr. Gorman answered. "I have a sick ewe out there. The veterinarian told me to watch her carefully, so I got to worrying and went out to see how she's getting along. He thinks she may be going to have twin lambs. Say, you kids are sort of late getting home, aren't you? Did you have any trouble with the station wagon?"

"No, sir, we didn't," Brian said. "It runs as smoothly as a Rolls Royce."

"And how many Rolls Royces have you driven?" Mart

asked, cramming a peanut butter sandwich into his mouth. He didn't expect an answer and got none.

"Then you didn't stop for something to eat, did you? Mary left enough food out for all Rivervale High School."

"No, Mr. Gorman," Trixie said. "This is what happened." She told him, very dramatically, about the bargain lambs for the barbecue.

"You say they told Ned they had frozen-food lockers in Valley Park—these men who sold the lambs to the committee?" Mr. Gorman asked.

"Yes, they did," Trixie said. "Are there any in Valley Park?"

"Of course there are," Mr. Gorman said, laughing, "and, of course, it was the Schwarz brothers you were trying to track down. They not only have food lockers, but they also make the best sausage this side of Pennsylvania. Say, Trixie, are you sure they didn't have bushy black beards? You know, Ned, she almost had your father behind bars the day before yesterday. It was a pretty close thing!"

Trixie was indignant. Mr. Gorman insisted upon treating everything she did as a joke. "Why, then," she asked slowly and pointedly, "did they drive into the woods late at night?"

"The answer to that is that they didn't drive into the woods at all," Mr. Gorman said. "Brian just said that maybe he made a mistake following them when he got to where the road turns off into the woods. Army Post

Road goes right on into Valley Park, where the Schwarz brothers live."

"*I* don't think Brian made any mistake following them. I was watching pretty carefully," Trixie said with great dignity.

"Ho, ho, ho!" Mr. Gorman's hearty laugh filled the room. "First thing you know, you'll have *me* arrested, Trixie, for stealing our own sheep. Stay away from those woods, though, all of you, if you want to get back to Sleepyside all in one piece. Good night, kids. Good night, Trixie. Let your uncle and Sheriff Brown and me worry about the sheep."

He went up the stairs.

"That's some good advice," Mart said. "Why can't we just have a good time on this one occasion, without you wearing your Schoolgirl Shamus badge?"

It was one thing for Jim to call Trixie "Schoolgirl Shamus." She sort of liked it, because he said it . . . well, in a sort of *liking* way. But the way Mart said it made her furious clear through.

"That's just enough from you, Mart Belden," she said. "Go on and eat, all of you. I'm going to bed. But the day is coming, and very, very soon, when you'll be eating your words, all of you, instead of sandwiches and potato chips. *I'm* going to find those thieves! You'll see!"

At the Skating Rink • 11

AT THE BREAKFAST TABLE, Trixie was quiet. She was quiet even when Ben's eyes twinkled and he pretended to slink away from her as she came down the stairs.

Mr. Gorman has told Ben about last night, she thought. *I don't see how they can joke so much about it. Uncle Andrew didn't think it was any joke. Neither did Mr. and Mrs. Gorman when we first came here. I guess it's my work he thinks is a joke. I've got to find those thieves, even if Honey isn't any help.*

It made Trixie sad to think that Honey wasn't more interested in helping her. *Anyone could have made that mistake I did about Mr. Schulz. Heavens, that's Ned's father,* she thought. *What on earth does he want with a black bushy beard? Well, I suppose Ned thinks I'm some kind of a freak, too. Oh, dear!*

Ned came in after they had finished breakfast. Mrs. Gorman gave him a cup of coffee and some of her doughnuts.

"How about everybody going skating this afternoon?" he asked. "We have a neat indoor rink over at River-vale. Some great skaters, too."

"We're going to help Mr. Gorman and Ben," Jim told him. "There are some fences that have to be mended over near the creek."

"The water there is so high," Brian added, "that Mr. Gorman is afraid the sheep will stray into it and drown."

"You don't need to stay home and help us," Mr. Gorman said quickly. "Ben and I can take care of it easily. Mr. Belden wanted you to have fun on your vacation."

"It's fun to help you," Mart said.

"He wants to tell everyone back at school that he's the fencing champion of Polk County, Iowa," Trixie said. "And he won't explain to them that it isn't done with foils, either."

Mart looked sheepish. There were times when Trixie almost read his mind. "I guess it's because we're almost twins," Trixie had told him once. If they had been twins, they probably would have gotten along much better. Mart's eleven-month seniority seemed to make him think he should dictate to Trixie, and when he tried it,

111

it made her see red every time.

"The rink is closed tomorrow," Ben said. "We don't really need help on the fences. You'd better go skating when you have the chance. The week is slipping by."

"No," Ned said. "Let's help first. I'll help, too, and maybe we can get enough done so we *can* go skating this afternoon. Some of the gang you met last night called me this morning to see if I couldn't get you to come."

"Jim had a call, too," Brian teased, "from a certain blond girl."

Trixie looked up sharply. She hadn't known that.

"I told her I couldn't show up," Jim said. "We'd all planned to do this work with Mr. Gorman and Ben."

"Oh, she'll keep," Ned said. "She'll be there. Dot is one of our star skaters. Anyway, these guys who called me were a lot more interested in having Trixie and Honey and Diana come than they were in having Mart and Brian."

"That figures," Mart said.

"Mart's a speed skater," Diana said proudly.

"That calls for a river or a lake," Ned said. "I'm glad he won't have a chance to show us up."

"Trixie and Honey do a figure skating act that's a wow," Mart said.

Ned whistled. "Maybe I'd better recall the invitation, then. Especially after the performance you Bob-Whites put on at the gym. We can't let the East get ahead of the Midwest again."

"We have a lot more ice—lakes and rivers—in West-chester County," Honey said. "It's colder there for a longer time in the spring, and we have more chance to practice, I guess, than you do here."

"Why don't you just wait and see how the Iowans skate?" Ben said. "Come on, let's get started for the creek."

The boys followed Mr. Gorman and Ben out to the barn to get the equipment for the fences. Just before he closed the door, Ned called back, "My father grew that beard, Trixie, for a Valley Park centennial celebration. When it was over, he just kept the beard for a while to tease my mother. He was scared when I told him how near he came to ending up in the hoosegow."

Well, Trixie thought, *so he does think I'm nothing but a joke.*

"It's mean of everyone to make fun of you so," Honey said. "And, Trixie, I honestly believe those men we saw last night *have* been stealing your uncle's sheep."

"You *do?*" Trixie said and hugged Honey tight. "I thought all kinds of mean, silly things about you, Honey. I thought everyone had abandoned me, for sure."

"I'm your partner; don't you remember?" Honey asked. "But I really *did* think you sort of jumped to con-clusions with Mr. Schulz," she continued. "And if you'd had a chance to know Ben as you do now, you would never have suspected him."

113

"To a detective, everyone is a suspect," Trixie said professionally. "Well, maybe I was in too much of a hurry. But, Honey, today is Thursday. That leaves only Friday and Saturday. And I do wish so much that I could have today free to do some more work on this case."

"Well, you can't," Honey said. "But let's not plan anything for tomorrow, and let's you and I just tell the others we're going to do exactly what we want to do for the day."

"The trouble is, we'll have to do it on foot if we tell them that," Trixie said. "I'm going to have a talk with Jim. At least *he* knows some of the things we've done in the past, and he may help."

While the boys were out in the fields, Honey, Trixie, and Diana busied themselves with several things. First they helped Mrs. Gorman do the breakfast dishes and dust the house. Then they washed some lingerie and manicured their fingernails. Diana put her hair up on rollers, but Trixie just wet the comb and drew it through her tangled curls. Honey's long hair was straight and shining.

"Wasn't Dan smart to ask your mother to send our skates?" Honey said. "Let's get them out of the box now. Hey, she sent them airmail special delivery! We could almost have bought new skates for what it cost to send them that way."

"Yes, and remember what Ben said about the special delivery part of it," Diana said, laughing.

114

"He said that just meant that Pop Wilson had to go to all the trouble of honking his horn when he left the package at the R.F.D. box down at the bottom of Sand Hill," Trixie said. "Moms will laugh at that, but she should have remembered that we don't get special delivery packages at Crabapple Farm, either."

"It was good of her to send them," Honey said. "It'll be a lot better to have our own skates than to rent or borrow them."

"Girls!" Mrs. Gorman called up the stairs. "It's time for lunch. The boys are coming in from the field. I guess they'll shower first out in the barn apartment and then come in. Do you want to help me get some food ready?"

The Bob-Whites had their first surprise when they saw the rink in Rivervale. "It's as big as the Arena in White Plains!" Trixie said. "And look at the crowd!"

"Yes, and then look at us, in blue jeans," Honey said. "Most of the girls are wearing skating costumes. There's Dot, waving to us. Doesn't she look like a dream?"

Trixie's heart skipped a beat. Dot *did* look like a dream. Her short skirt was creamy white, and her pullover sweater matched. Both were embroidered in gay Bavarian designs. Her blond hair was topped by a Tyrolean cap. All the other Rivervale girls looked almost as attractive.

"They must really make a business of skating here," Jim said to Ned.

"A lot of us belong to the Des Moines Figure Skating

115

Club," Ned explained. "We have a Danish teacher. He's pretty keen."

"If they skate as well as they dress for the rink, we're sunk," Trixie mourned. Dot was clinging to Jim's arm, leading him into the building. Trixie looked down woefully at her jeans and her loose red sweater. "Moms *could* have sent our costumes," she told Honey and Diana.

"I suppose she may have thought we wouldn't want to look different from the other girls here," Honey said.

"We really do look different, but not in the way she may have thought," Diana said. "What do we care? Trixie, you and Honey skate so beautifully. And the boys are whizzes on the ice. Let's just make the best of it."

That's easy for you to say, Trixie thought to herself. *Honey and Di look beautiful in any old kind of costume. They aren't competing with girls like Dot, either.*

Inside the building, a jukebox played. Out on the ice, couples skated around the rink, easily and gracefully, in time to the music.

Boys from Rivervale High crowded around Honey, Diana, and Trixie, helping them adjust their skates. At first Trixie waved them off, but when she saw Honey and Diana accepting help as though they had never seen a skate before, she changed her own tactics. *I've got to quit being such a tomboy*, she thought and smiled quickly in gratitude as Ned laced her skates for her . . . loose around the toes, pulled tight near the ankle, and loose again at the top. Then he slipped some rubber guards over the blades so Trixie could walk across the wood floor to the ice.

Over by the jukebox, a man in Danish costume—the coach Ned had mentioned—turned off the music and took up a megaphone to make an announcement.

"We have visitors here from New York," he said. "They are members of a club called the Bob-Whites of the Glen, in Westchester County, New York. They have just staged a very successful ice carnival in their city, for the benefit of the Central American earthquake victims. We hope they will now give us a demonstration of some of their skating. Most of you saw them during the warm-up period at the gym last night. If they skate as well as they hit the basket, we'll have to surrender the Des Moines Club Trophy. First, Miss Honey Wheeler and Miss Trixie Belden."

"Oh, *no*," Honey said under her breath to Trixie. "We just can't do it. They shouldn't ask us. All these people watching. Trixie, we had to practice days and days for the carnival. I don't even remember what we're supposed to do."

"Well, remember fast!" Trixie hissed. "Ned must have put them up to this. He should have said something to us, to give us a chance to refuse. We *have* to do it, Honey. We just *have* to."

Honey, inspired by Trixie's courage and determination, bent and slipped the rubber guards from her skates. "What do we do first?" she asked desperately.

"Around the rink a few times just skating," Trixie said, "hand in hand. Then the spiral glide. I'll take the boy's part."

Honey stumbled as they started out. "Chin up!" Trixie commanded her. Then they swung into a long, easy glide to the music. "There, that's better. Around the rink once more. . . ."

Determinedly Trixie guided Honey through all their pet exhibition dancing—figure eights, forward outside figure eights, the bunny hop, and, finally, a ballet jump.

The crowd applauded excitedly as they finished.

"They're just being polite," Honey said. "We never looked worse. On that snowplow stop, I leaned so far forward I was lucky not to fall on my face."

"Whatever you do, don't act the way you feel," Trixie said. "Bow, smile, wave. There, thank goodness that's over." They sat down on the bench.

"That was excellent," the Danish instructor called through the megaphone. "Thank you, girls. No wonder the carnival was so great a success. Now we will let our visitors rest for a while, and Dot Murray will give an exhibition of figure skating."

It was an exhibition all three girls from Westchester County, and the three boys, too, wouldn't forget for a long time. Jim led Dot across the board floor and removed her skate guards for her. On the ice, she stood tall, poised, and graceful. She laughingly kissed her hand to the audience, then to Jim.

Trixie's heart hit the top of her stomach with a dull

thud. Then she completely forgot her unfamiliar jealousy as she watched the lovely figure in white dance around and around the rink, in perfect time to the music. She did everything the girls had done, and more, and did it far better. Her ballet steps were perfectly timed and exquisitely executed. When she ended her performance with a series of Arabian cartwheels, Trixie clapped so vigorously she almost fell off the bench.

"She's good, isn't she?" Jim asked, crowding down on the bench next to Trixie.

"She's out of this world! She's unbelievable! And isn't she perfectly beautiful?"

Jim nodded. "Yes, she is, Trixie. And do you know something else? I know a girl who's the best sport in these United States. I saw you falter when Honey didn't want to go out on the ice. Then I saw your head go up. That's it, Trixie! They can't beat courage, no matter how well they skate."

Jim left her then, to lead Dot back over the board floor. Trixie's heart sang. The whole world was sunny again—so sunny she didn't realize for a while what had happened when Ned sat down by her and spoke to her.

"You sure goofed again, Trixie," he said.

"What do you mean?" Trixie asked, her eyes starry. "I couldn't ever hope to skate as well as Dot does. She's a professional right now, whether she realizes it or not."

Ned waved his hand in a gesture of frustration. "I didn't mean that, Trixie. Forget skating for a while."

"What are you talking about, then?"

"Just this: I called the principal and told him that we thought there was a good chance the lambs we used last night had been stolen. Do you know what he said?"

Trixie's eyes questioned.

"He gave me one of the worst tongue-lashings I've ever had in my life. He said that he himself had arranged with the committee for the purchase of the lambs; that they had been bought from the Schwarz brothers, who own a locker in Valley Park, just the way Mr. Gorman said; that if I said another word to anyone about the meat for the Rivervale High School barbecue having been stolen meat, he'd arrange proper censure. Boy, did he hand it to me!"

"But—but—you said they offered the lambs at a bargain," Trixie said.

"They did. I was there when they did. I didn't hear anyone call the men by name. I didn't know them. I don't hang around food lockers. But Mr. Gorman guessed who they were right away when we told him about it last night, remember? Boy, you certainly made a rumpus about nothing!"

"Why, Ned Schulz," Trixie said, "how can you talk that way? You live here. You should have known. You should have told me."

"I've only lived here a year. You must be *some* detective, suspecting everyone you see. . . ."

"I just wish you could talk to the sheriff of Westchester County and the chief of police! They could tell you a few things about what I've done. Furthermore, what business would any honest men have going off into Walnut Woods that late at night and—"

"Ben said there are two roads that seem to go into Walnut Woods," Ned said. "One is a dead-end road. I don't know where the other one goes. The Schwarz brothers must have turned off at Army Post Road, and we lost them in the dark. They were the same men we bought the lambs from . . . the ones we started to follow in that truck."

"It isn't *that* truck I'm interested in anymore," Trixie said. "There must be another one—one that's been going down the other road to a hideout in Walnut Woods. You'll find out, Ned Schulz . . . that *was* stolen meat that was used at the barbecue. Maybe the Schwarz brothers didn't steal it. I suppose they didn't. But what was to prevent them from buying it from some men who *have* been operating around here, stealing sheep and selling them cheap to lockers? Maybe the Schwarz brothers saw a chance to make a little easy money—"

"Trixie," Ned said, "you knock me dead! You make up your mind to something, and nothing can change it. Right?"

"Just remember this, Ned. There's *something* queer going on back there in that woods. And I intend to find out what it is."

Jim's and Brian's skating redeemed the Bob-Whites. The crowd, too, had many complimentary things to say about Honey and Trixie's performance.

Trixie's mind wasn't on any of it. "Tomorrow," she muttered, "and Saturday . . . that's all the time left to solve the mystery for Uncle Andrew. I *know* I'm on the right track. I *have* to be!"

However, when the Bob-Whites had returned to Happy Valley Farm and eaten their dinner, something happened that drove all thought of the stolen sheep far from Trixie's mind.

Poor Little Orphan · 12

MR. GORMAN WASN'T at the dinner table. Self-conscious about having made a third mistake, Trixie was glad of it. She wouldn't have to listen to any more teasing. It had been bad enough having Mart and the other Bob-Whites keep reminding her that their trip the night before had just been another wild-goose chase.

I'd wish the earth could open and swallow me up, or that somehow I could vanish from here and find myself back at Crabapple Farm. I'd wish that, Trixie said to herself, *except that I'm not going to quit now.*

"A penny for your thoughts," Jim offered quietly. "You're dreaming, Trixie. Your mind must have been miles away."

"Not really," Trixie said. "I'm just sorry Honey and I had to put on that crazy performance at the skating rink this afternoon."

"It wasn't that bad," Jim assured her. "It wasn't bad at all. It's that Dot had to follow you right away. A person just can't do everything perfectly. . . ."

"I know that, Jim. Wasn't she marvelous? Just like a poem. I never saw anything more beautiful. Honestly, though, that isn't what I mind so much. I just hate to have wasted all that time at the rink."

"It could have been just fun, Trixie. That's what we're supposed to be doing here—having fun. And I'd like to have Dot see you on Satan's Baby. He's well named. I'll bet she couldn't stay on him two minutes."

Trixie laughed happily. "You're wonderful, Jim," she said. "I suppose I *can* ride, but maybe Dot can ride just as well. What I mean about wasting time is that I made another boo-boo trying to track down those thieves. Now it's Thursday night. Jim, will you go with me to Walnut Woods tonight and try again to see where that flickering light is?"

"I will not!" Jim said decisively. Then, as Trixie's face fell, he added, "I'll go with you tomorrow, though, Trixie. What's the use of going back there again at night? We were there once in pitch-darkness and had to back out. Wait till tomorrow."

"Then we'll waste this whole evening. I wonder where Mr. Gorman is. Did anyone hear where he is?" Trixie asked Honey, who sat at her side.

"Some trouble out in the field," Brian answered from across the table. "Ben's gone out to see what's delaying him."

"Do you suppose more of the sheep are missing?" Trixie asked anxiously.

"If they are, you can take your bird-dog nose off the ground," Mart said. "You've missed the scent too often."

"It isn't anything about stolen sheep," Mrs. Gorman said. "It's just that ewe he's been watching so carefully— the one who's going to have twin lambs. We've been trying to call the veterinarian. He doesn't answer. The operator thinks his phone is out of order. And that ewe is liable to have her lambs at any moment."

"How can you tell?" Diana asked, wide-eyed.

"You couldn't make a mistake," Mrs. Gorman said. "When a lamb is about to be born, the ewe stops grazing and runs about, calling to her baby. She doesn't know it hasn't been born yet, and she nuzzles other lambs, looking for her own. It's sort of pathetic. Here come my husband and Ben now."

"Did you get hold of the veterinarian?" Mr. Gorman asked, closing the door behind him.

"He doesn't answer," Mrs. Gorman told him, and she explained that the telephone might be out of order.

"Then I'd better go over to his house and get him," Ben said, "or we'll lose the ewe *and* the lambs."

"We'll lose them anyway, Ben," Mr. Gorman said resignedly. "There just isn't time to wait any longer. She has to have help. I'll go out again, Mary," he told

125

his wife, "and see what I can do."

"Do you think I could help?" Brian asked.

"He's going to be a doctor," Honey explained.

"No, thanks. I don't think you can do a thing," Mr. Gorman said.

"He helped at home when our calf was born," Trixie said quickly. "And at Honey's house, too, when one of their mares foaled. I can help, too," she added, "because I helped Brian both times. I'm a volunteer helper at the hospital."

"Trixie Belden, you can't—" Diana said, amazed.

"Oh, yes, I can!" Trixie insisted and got up from the table. "Come on, Brian. Mr. Gorman, please let Ben go for the veterinarian, and we'll help you."

Mr. Gorman threw up his hands in resignation. "I can't lose," he said. "Go ahead, Ben. Come on, kids."

Mrs. Gorman thrust a quickly made sandwich into her husband's hand, and he went out, munching it.

When they got to the barn, they found that the ewe had made a nest for herself in some hay in the corner of the big stall room. She looked up at them with her gentle eyes and bleated softly. Close beside her lay two little newborn lambs, one of them rather yellow and the other coal black.

"There, there . . . quiet now," Mr. Gorman said and put his hand on the ewe's head. "You just went ahead and took care of things yourself, didn't you? We have to work fast," he said quickly to Brian and Trixie. "If she doesn't claim them right away, she won't ever do it. There, there now," he said softly.

"Help me, Brian—help to get them started feeding." He took the yellowish lamb and guided its mouth to the mother. She turned and sniffed the homely little thing, all ears and head. Then she uttered a sound she hadn't made for a year . . . a low rumble in her throat, without opening her mouth. The little lamb, tasting its mother's warm milk, bleated happily and snuggled close, feeding.

"She's taken that one all right," Mr. Gorman said with relief. "Now, Trixie, the little black one."

Trixie took the black lamb, all wrinkles and loose skin, and handed it to Mr. Gorman.

The poor baby bleated pitifully. The mother listened, sniffed it, and, as it tried to feed, bunted it cruelly.

"You *bad* mother!" Trixie said.

"It's natural with a twin," Mr. Gorman said. "Let's try her again."

"Let me," Brian said. He dipped his finger in a few drops of warm milk from the little white lamb's busy mouth, then rubbed it over the small black face.

The mother sniffed again, then bunted it away, angrily and finally. Clearly, she wanted nothing to do with it.

"It's just no use," Mr. Gorman said. "We're stuck with an orphan lamb. Let's get up to the house in a hurry and take care of it. It can't live long this way. It has to be fed as soon as possible."

127

"I'll take care of things here," Brian said, "and see that the mother is comfortable. She should have something to eat, too, shouldn't she?"

"Yes," Mr. Gorman said, "thanks for thinking of it. Take some of that hot water we brought in the bucket, Brian, and mix with it some of that feed there. Make a sort of warm mash. Sheep love warm mash. Just leave it in that pan there beside her. She'll eat it when the lamb stops feeding.

"We haven't had a black lamb born in several years," Mr. Gorman told Trixie on the way to the house. "Some people think they're bad luck. I don't. The only trouble is, so many of the mothers won't claim a black one."

"I'd a thousand times rather have a black lamb than that yellowish thing," Trixie said.

"The mother wouldn't," Mr. Gorman said. "That's the color all white lambs are when they're born. They quickly turn white. Here we are, Trixie. Take this baby, please, while I open the door."

Mrs. Gorman and the other Bob-Whites waited for Mr. Gorman, Trixie, and Brian in the warm kitchen. When Mrs. Gorman saw the lamb in Trixie's arms, she hurried to warm some milk. "Oh, no," she said, "not another orphan! Did the ewe die, Hank?"

Mr. Gorman shook his head, smiled, and held up two fingers. "Twins," he said. "Everything all right except . . . well, she wouldn't own the black one. Guess you're in for a season of bottles and nipples, Mary."

Hastily Mrs. Gorman turned on the oven. "Keep

128

holding the lamb while I fill the bottle," she told Trixie.

"Now, then, put the lamb in the oven," she said, opening the oven door.

"It's too hot," Trixie said. "The lamb will be burned!"

"It can't be *too* hot," Mrs. Gorman said. "Quick, Trixie, please."

Reluctantly Trixie surrendered the orphan to the hot oven and left the door open, as Mrs. Gorman instructed her.

Mrs. Gorman held the lamb's small head, then watched the baby relax in the warmth of the oven, stop struggling, and, with a big sigh, start feeding from the bottle, its tiny corkscrew tail jerking in happiness.

Ben came in and with him Brian. "Brian told me it's all over, and everything's all right," he said to Mr. Gorman. "It's a good thing. The veterinarian wasn't at home."

"Everything's done, thanks to Brian and Trixie," Mr. Gorman said. "But we'll have an orphan to feed all summer. Five times a day, then three times a day," he explained to the Bob-Whites, "and so on, all summer long."

"Lambing season's early this year," Ben said. "It had started in Ames when I was there. Say, if you think that little white lamb is ugly, Trixie, you should see one of the Rambouillet lambs . . . all skin, big ears, and wobbly legs."

"They're all darling, anyway," Honey said. "Listen to the way it's going after that bottle!"

129

"Ben usually has the job of taking care of the orphans," Mrs. Gorman said. "He's a sort of substitute mother . . . at least the lambs think so. They follow him around everyplace."

"I don't encourage it," Ben said and turned bright red.

"No, but you have every bit as good a time as the lambs do," Mrs. Gorman said. "Ben jumps and plays with them," she told the Bob-Whites. "If Trixie keeps on feeding this one, it'll run after her, too. How'd you like to be a lamb's mother, Trixie?"

"If they were born about a week old, I wouldn't mind at all," Trixie said. "But not one of those little yellow things . . . ugh!"

"She won't have to bother about being the black one's mother," Ben said. "That big ewe you bought from Mr. Schulz last year is ready to drop her lamb most anytime. If she does tomorrow, maybe we can get her to mother the black one, too."

"I doubt it," Mr. Gorman said. "We'd better not count on it. There isn't much we can do. If the black lamb's own mother wouldn't claim it, there isn't much chance the other ewe will."

"Not unless her own lamb is born dead," Ben said. "It happened last year."

"I hope it doesn't happen this year," Mrs. Gorman said. "It's a busy time of year," she said to the Bob-Whites. "I guess any time of year on a farm is a busy time. But I like the spring most of all. Birds nesting, lambs underfoot everywhere—they're the most playful and lovable little animals in the world—wild flowers popping out," she went on, "Johnny-jump-ups down by the creek, purple violets, Dutchman's-breeches, carpets of spring beauties, purple iris in the gully. . . ."

"Later on," Mr. Gorman said, "purple vervain and then black-eyed Susans and wild roses. . . ."

"Iowa is a beautiful place," Mrs. Gorman said contentedly, almost to herself.

"We have pretty wild flowers at home, too," Trixie said.

"I'm sure you have," Mrs. Gorman said. "It's a beautiful country we live in. Even the desert blooms."

Mart, remembering the Christmas the Bob-Whites spent at a dude ranch in Arizona, nodded vigorously. "Jeepers," he said, "the desert at night! You can't beat it. Not even out here at Happy Valley Farm, where the stars are so bright."

"You can reach up and pick them out of the sky in Arizona," Diana said, "or you think you can."

Jim smiled, remembering. "The little calves out there —the ranch was full of them—are some of the cutest little things in the whole world."

"All locoed," Ben laughed. "They can't stand up."

"I guess," Mr. Gorman said, "the good Lord intended people to love the young of any animal—even man's, and he's the orneriest of all animals—because there never was a young one born of bird or beast that you didn't first laugh at and then give your heart to.

131

"Let the dogs in, please," he told Brian, when he heard them scratching at the door. "Tip and Tag take advantage of us," he added. "They know we're crazy about them, don't they, Mary?" He pulled gently at the dogs' ears as the big, awkward things tried to climb up in his lap.

"We're softies, I guess," Mrs. Gorman said. "But these young ones are, too," she added. "Look at them. Every one has a kitten or a lamb in his lap. Every one but Jim, and see what he drew!"

Tag, after vainly trying to crowd himself into the same chair with Jim, finally managed to pull his big bulk up onto Jim's lap and rest his right front leg around Jim's shoulder.

Trixie, watching, sighed happily. She was tired. It had been a hard day—a long day. Tomorrow would be even harder. Tomorrow she meant, somehow, to repay Uncle Andrew for this fabulous week. She intended to go with Jim into Walnut Woods and, if she were lucky, come up with an answer to the problem of the missing sheep. There wasn't much time left.

The Great Rabbit Hunt · 13

WHAT ARE WE going to call the orphan?" Diana asked as they crowded into the big kitchen after a brisk run on the horses.

"Hercules, I'd suggest," Mart said. "Look at the size of him, will you! He must have grown double during the night."

The black lamb, in a child's playpen in the corner of the kitchen, frisked with the kittens, pawing at them with his nimble feet.

"Midnight would be a good name, I think," Honey said. "Every time I'd get to sleep, I'd hear Trixie's alarm clock buzz and hear her going down the stairs to warm some milk."

"Midnight's a perfect name," Trixie said and blew a kiss to her little pet.

"Every two hours Trixie came downstairs to feed him," Mrs. Gorman said, "just as faithful as could be. First I tried to stop her, but then I was so tired, I just left it all to her."

"He nearly knocked the bottle out of my hand, he was so hungry. I hope Mr. Gorman will have some luck getting Midnight adopted," Trixie said. "Or has the new lamb been born?"

"It was born early this morning," Mrs. Gorman said, "and it didn't live. Hank tried his best to pass Midnight off in its place, but it didn't work. You see," she went on, "if we work fast enough, sometimes we can put the skin of the stillborn lamb over the head and shoulders of the orphan and fool the ewe long enough for her to let it feed—then she'll adopt it. It's wonderful when it works."

"That's probably where Aesop got his idea for the wolf in sheep's clothing," Mart said. Everyone hooted at him, but he went on. "You can be pretty sure it wasn't Iowa farmers or the professors in the agricultural department at Iowa State University who invented the practice. There were sheep in the hills of Egypt and Jerusalem thousands of years ago."

"Don't get so worked up about it," Brian said. "Say, Mrs. Gorman, that creek out in the field is almost even with its banks. I couldn't get Black Giant to go near it. Horses are like babies about water."

"Ben said the river is up, too," Mrs. Gorman said, "and it's clouding over. Maybe we'll have some rain."

"We'd better get over to Walnut Woods right away," Trixie whispered to Jim. "Honey wants to go, too. And do you know something? I heard Mr. Gorman tell Mrs. Gorman before breakfast that he was going in and talk to Sheriff Brown today about that light in the woods. He said he was getting sick and tired of the way the police were stalling."

Jim whistled. "That's the first time Mr. Gorman has admitted that there might be something to a hideout in the woods, isn't it? We better get going now, Trixie— What's that Mrs. Gorman is saying?"

"Oh, no!" Trixie groaned. "Oh, no!"

"So I thought," Mrs. Gorman finished, "that you haven't planned to do anything in particular today, and as long as Ben and Hank thought it would be a good idea, I told Ned and the others to come along rabbit hunting with you. There they are now."

Ned Schulz and the Hubbell twins, Barbara and Bob, from Army Post Road, drove into the farmyard in Ned's new red car.

Mart, Diana, Brian, and Honey ran out to welcome them, while the dogs barked and snapped at the white-wall tires. The kittens, startled by all the noise, arched their backs indignantly.

"Oh, darn, darn, darn!" Trixie said to Jim. "Do you think we can duck out of it?"

"Not a chance," Jim said. "Didn't you hear what Mrs.

135

Gorman just said? Rabbit hunting! I wouldn't pass that up for thief hunting in a whole month of Sundays."

"Jim Frayne, you said you'd go with me today," Trixie reminded him.

"I will, too. Calm down, Trix. We have the whole day ahead of us. Heck, Trixie, I don't get a chance to go rabbit hunting every day. Ben said the rabbits around here are as big as kangaroos."

"I don't care if they're as big as elephants," Trixie said mournfully. "I'd never take a shot at one of them, anyway. I'd just as soon shoot the Easter bunny."

"Wait till you see," Ned said as he heard Trixie's last remark. "We never hit one. They're too quick. Most of the fun is hunting them out. Say, Jim, I brought another BB gun for you. BB shot wouldn't dent a jack-rabbit's skin, even if we did hit one," he added as the other girls added their protests to Trixie's.

"Come on with us," Brian begged. "We can have a lot of fun running races with the rabbits, at least. You've been wanting to get out in the fields of the farm. This is your chance."

"We won't stay long," Jim whispered to Trixie. "I'll keep my promise."

"And we'll leave the BB guns here if you don't like the idea," Ned told Trixie. "It's just as much fun without them."

So the girls put on their jeans and boots and heavy sweaters, tied scarves around their heads, and went with Barbara Hubbell and the boys.

"If you lost about half your kitchen garden every year to those thieving rabbits, you wouldn't feel so squeamish about shooting them," Mrs. Gorman called to the girls as they left.

"Take the dogs!" Ben called from the barn. Tip and Tag joined the group, barking excitedly, heads up and tails wagging.

Bob and Barbara Hubbell had sat near the Bob-Whites at the barbecue. Barbara was about Trixie's size, with coal black curls. Her twin was as tall as Brian. Trixie liked them both.

"They play guitars and sing," Ned told the Bob-Whites. "Maybe we can get them to perform for us when we get back."

Heavens, I hope not, Trixie thought. *I'll never get to Walnut Woods.*

Then, before she knew what was happening, she was having so much fun she forgot all about the sheep thieves.

The air was sharp with the chill of coming rain, just sharp enough to release pent-up energy. Dancing and shouting, singing at the top of their voices, the Bob-Whites, the twins, and Ned raced up the pasture slope. In the clumps of bushes that dotted the field and in the light woods that edged the land, Ben had told them, they might startle some jackrabbits.

The sheep were grazing in the far meadow, but when they heard the shouting, they retired to the outer edge by the fence.

"Guess it's just as well," Ned said when he saw them scattering. "Ben warned us not to frighten them. Hey— that bunch of brush over there—here, Tag! Here, Tip!"

The collies, seasoned rabbit chasers, didn't have to be told what to do. They crouched low, dragging themselves cautiously along as they approached the ring of brush.

"Get over there, Jim," Bob Hubbell called, "over there on the side. I'll beat the brush on this side with this stick. When he hops out, you grab him. Hey, Tag! Stop that!"

At the first stirring of the brush, Tag's ears went back. He barked. A rabbit—a big one—jumped out, close enough for Jim to touch his whiskers. But before Tag could make a move, the jackrabbit bunched his back legs, bounded high into the air, stretched himself full length to soar, and came down about eighteen feet away. He was off, flopping across the grass like an old hat in a high wind, three jumps ahead of the yipping dogs.

The dogs had sense enough to abandon the chase, and they came back, panting, to look for the next victim.

"Jeepers, I almost had that one by the leg; did you see me?" Jim called, his face glowing.

Trixie picked herself up, laughing, from where Tag had knocked her down when he saw the rabbit. "You didn't have a chance, Jim," she said. "Did you see the size of that jackrabbit?"

"Jackrabbits," Mart announced in a professional tone, "are two feet long when full-grown and weigh six to eight pounds."

"That one's ears alone were a foot long!" Trixie insisted.

"Keep to the truth," Brian warned. "I think jackrabbits belong to the rat family."

"That is a fallacy," Mart said. "They *used* to be called rodents."

"I like the little cottontails best," Diana said as she brushed herself off after her dash after the rabbit. "Are jackrabbits just grown-up cottontails?"

"Oh, Di!" Mart said disgustedly. "Are rats grown-up mice? I'm a Scout," he went on proudly. "And Jim and Brian should know about rabbits, too, if they've studied their manuals. A jackrabbit is entirely different from Peter Rabbit. The western kind is called *Lepus townsendii.*"

"I suppose the *Lepus* part comes from the big jumps they make," Diana said. "I wish I could remember things the way you do, Mart."

Mart made a deep bow to her. "My public!" he said. "I wish Trixie would take advantage of my superior brain and learn a few things from me."

"I want to choose the things I want to learn," Trixie said, "and not have them spouted at me all the time."

"Call a truce, you two," Jim said. "We have to keep quieter around the next clump. Down, Tag . . . Tip!" The dogs, at his command, slunk close to the ground and inched along toward the big brush pile ahead.

"Nothing stirring there, I guess," Bob said in a whisper. "I'll stay on this side . . . there . . . nothing, see?" Bob kicked the dense bushes and out hopped three jackrabbits!

Two of them got away, with Tip and Tag after them like arrows. The third one, the biggest, started to straighten for a long leap, moved toward Mart's side of the bushes, tacked, turned to Ned's side, and tacked again, bewildered.

"Get him!" Mart called. "There!"

"Where?" Brian called, hooting with laughter. "Look at him now, Mart! Watch out!"

The rabbit, desperate, threw himself forward, kicking like a mule with his powerful hind legs, and then, catching Mart off guard, sent him sprawling.

Tip and Tag came back, fuming with frustration, ready for a real fight. Mart, too, his appetite whetted by the near catch, ran at full speed toward a huge clump of dried grass. About twenty-five feet away, the dogs crouched to the ground, then slid along on their bellies. The Bob-Whites and others stood back to watch the dogs' strategy.

Slowly they worked their way through the stubble to the tufts of grass, then gave a sudden leap into the middle, yelping like mad. Out jumped a big jackrabbit, right under Tip's nose. In two bounds it was thirty feet away from the astonished dogs. It stopped, looked back tauntingly, wiggled its nose, and was off with the wind.

Tip and Tag just sat, dejected.

"If we only had a horse," Honey said.

"Do you think even a racehorse could catch a jack-rabbit?" Ned asked. "There isn't anything that can catch one of them. We ought to have a couple of good shotguns."

"That's not sportsmanlike," Trixie said.

"Nuts!" Mart said. "It's good sportsmanship for one of them to kick me in the stomach and knock me down, I suppose. Come, Tag."

They had been working down the field at the edge of the gully. Tip and Tag, acting strangely, sniffed along the ground, following a trail toward the corner of the pasture.

"They're after something," Ned said. "Quiet; let's follow them."

The dogs, yipping, their tails going like windmills, scratched frantically at the ground in the far corner of the Belden acres, routing out a group of sheep that seemed to be feeding greedily on something.

"If it's another rabbit they're after, count me out," Diana said, dropping to the ground, exhausted from running and laughing. "I'm bushed."

"Me, too," Barbara said.

"Maybe the dogs have found a rabbit burrow," Trixie wondered out loud.

"There you go," Mart said. "Rabbits—that is, jack-rabbits—don't have burrows."

"Just happy wanderers?" Trixie asked.

"Nope. They make nests on top of the ground for their young and—"

"And, Mr. Encyclopedia?" Trixie asked, waiting.

"And the baby jackrabbits are left there to more or less fend for themselves. They're born with heavy fur and with their eyes open. Cottontails are born blind, naked, and helpless."

"But the cottontail mothers take good care of their babies for months," Barbara said. "The jackrabbits shove their children out in the world after just a few days."

"I think it's pretty smart of Mart to know all that stuff," Diana said. "He's always the one of the Bob-Whites who can tell us about everything."

"That's right," Brian agreed. "You don't give him credit for storing up all that knowledge, Trixie."

"Oh, yes, I do," Trixie said, smiling. "I just can't let his ego run away with him."

"Oh, yes?" Mart said. "Say, what do you suppose those dogs are doing? They're making a big fuss about something."

Trixie jumped up from the ground. "If it's a nest of baby rabbits," she said, "I'd love to have one."

"Mrs. Gorman wouldn't let you take it near the house," Barbara said, getting up from the ground and brushing off her jeans.

"Gosh, it's no nest of baby rabbits," Jim said. "Listen to Tag! Have they found a snake?"

"Could be," Bob said. "Newborn snakes come out in the sun in the spring and warm themselves. One time

142

Barbara and I killed four rattlesnakes in our pasture—just killed them with stones."

The dogs, who had been racing around a small circle of ground in the far corner, pawing and scratching, jumping into the air and pawing again, now began to run in wider circles. Tag howled like a lost soul and, tail between his legs, ran as though a thousand demons were right behind him.

"What is it, fella?" Jim called, running toward him. "What's bothering you?"

"Look at the air back of you, and you'll soon see," Bob called. "Run for your life! They've dug up a bumblebee nest! Run!" He took Honey's hand and pushed his sister, Barbara, ahead of him. "Run!"

"They've nipped Tag on the nose," Jim said. "Come on, Trixie."

Trixie, who had waited to see if she could help Tag, found herself pulled along in a stumbling dead run. The dogs were far ahead, howling so loudly that they brought Mrs. Gorman out of the house.

"It's starting to rain," Bob called back to the Bob-Whites. "That'll slow down the bees. Boy, is it pouring down!"

"What on earth happened?" Mrs. Gorman asked as she held the door wide to let the rabbit hunters tumble into the kitchen.

"Tag—bee stung him on the nose—bumblebee," Trixie gasped. "Poor old Tag!"

"Did they sting any of you?" Mrs. Gorman asked

143

anxiously, at the same time reaching into the cupboard for a box of soda.

"They couldn't catch us," Trixie said, laughing and still out of breath. "What a nose poor old Tag has!"

The collie lay on the floor in the corner of the big kitchen, pawing at his sore nose, which had doubled in size.

"I'll help you," Trixie said, her laughter turned to pity at the poor dog's plight. "Good old Tag! Are you making a poultice?" she asked Mrs. Gorman.

"Here it is." Mrs. Gorman handed Trixie a cloth soaked in warm water and soda. "You'll have to keep it on his nose," she said. "If you can keep it there for about ten minutes, it'll take the sting away, and the swelling will start to go down."

Tag moaned and licked Trixie's hand but let her keep the poultice on his poor nose. Tip, restless, walked around and around Tag, seeming to sense something wrong.

"There, now," Mrs. Gorman said. "Thank goodness there was no more harm done than that. I've seen Hank and Ben pretty sick from beestings. Heavens, I'd better stir around and get something for you to eat. You're probably starved."

Ned snapped his fingers. "Am I a dumb bunny!" he said. "I forgot to say that Mom has a picnic lunch waiting for us over at our house. She told me to tell you that as soon as I came, Mrs. Gorman, and I forgot. Gee, I hope you haven't gone and cooked a lot of things."

"I haven't," Mrs. Gorman assured him. "I've been so busy all morning. I had to sort of clean up the kitchen and put Midnight's playpen away. Ben took him out to the barn and, well, with one thing and another. . . ."

"Good!" Ned said. "Mom has a lot of food waiting . . . even cherry pies."

"Say no more; I'm dying," Mart said, holding his stomach.

"I guess we're all hungry," Honey said. "It's a grand idea, Ned."

"It sure is pouring down now!" Bob exclaimed.

"We can crowd into my car," Ned said. "It'll hold all of you till we get across the road and down to our house, anyway. We'll eat and then roll up the rug and dance. I've got some neat country western records."

"I sure can't think of a better way to spend a rainy afternoon!" said Mart.

"*I* can," Trixie whispered to Jim.

"So can I," Honey, who heard her, whispered.

"Have a heart!" Jim answered. "Look at the rain come down!"

"And remember, this is Friday," Trixie hissed. "You promised."

"All right, all right," Jim murmured, resigned. "What are we going to tell Ned?"

"Leave it to me," Trixie answered.

"We'll just have to eat and run, Jim and Honey and I," she told Ned. "We have to go to the airport and pick up our reservations for Sunday."

145

"Jeepers!" Brian said. "I forgot. I'll go with you, Jim, and let the girls stay in out of the rain. Better yet, why can't we just call the airport?"

"I'm not made of sugar," Trixie said quickly, "and neither is Honey. Anyway, we have some shopping to do in the airport gift shop."

"Important enough to go out in a cloudburst for?" Brian asked.

"Yes," Trixie and Honey answered together.

"Okay," Brian said. "Don't say I didn't offer."

"Don't say I *did!*" Mart chimed in. "Come on, gang, let's get to Ned's house. Better bring your jackets. It's still raining. Boy, am I hungry!"

Dinner With the Schulzes • 14

NED'S RED CAR, crowded almost beyond its capacity with nine young people, turned onto the winding road that led from Army Post Road to Seven Oaks, Ned Schulz's home.

The house was built of brick, a pre-Civil War home, remodeled and modernized. When the car stopped, Ned's two German shepherd dogs, who looked almost as tall as the car itself, wagged their huge bodies to show how glad they were that their master and his friends had come.

"They're beauties," Jim said, making friends immediately as Ned introduced the dogs to each one of them, laying his hand on each shoulder as he did.

"If I didn't do that," Ned said, "they might try to protect me from you. I've had them six years. Once, when we lived in Evanston, they saved my life . . . in Lake Michigan."

Ned put his head down close to the big dogs' heads and whispered to them, stroking their necks and tugging at their ears.

"It makes me lonesome for Reddy," Trixie said. "He's our red Irish setter. He really belongs to the whole family. Jim has a black and white springer called Patch. He sort of belongs to all of us Beldens and Bob-Whites, too."

Ned had stopped the car under an old-fashioned porte cochere. The rain still came down in buckets, but here they were sheltered for the moment and could look about. The grounds of the Schulz home were elaborate and beautifully tended. A row of evergreens lined the curved driveway, and an old ornamental iron fence enclosed what must be a lovely formal garden in the summertime. In back of the patio, they could see a large oval swimming pool, boarded over now for the winter.

"We'll go in here," Ned said and opened the door from the porte cochere. "Mom is probably in the kitchen helping with the food. She does most of our cooking, and my mom can really fry chicken."

A long redwood table had been brought from the patio into the big old-fashioned kitchen. Down the center of the table were arranged huge platters of golden fried chicken, casseroles of scalloped potatoes, a large pot of baked beans, and two large wooden bowls of tossed salad. There were baskets of buttered buns and huge plates of cookies and the promised cherry pies—and, over all, there was a delicious country-kitchen fragrance.

And, of course, there was Ned's mom.

She didn't look much older than Ned himself. She wore a yellow sweater and a tan skirt, and she had black curly hair and a warm welcoming smile. It wasn't until she walked toward them that the Bob-Whites noticed a decided limp.

"Polio," Barbara whispered to Trixie. "Isn't she just wonderful?"

Within a few minutes, the laughing group was seated around the table, all talking at once. All of them, too, were immediately in love with Ned's pretty mother.

"Tell me more," she said, "about the Bob-Whites of the Glen. The United Nations Children's Fund has been a vital interest of mine since its beginning. Have you kept your interest in it since the antique show?"

"Yes, we have," Trixie answered. "We sell their stationery all around Westchester County. Really, it practically sells itself, it's so attractive."

Mrs. Schulz nodded. "I use it, too."

"We already have orders for cards for next Christmas," Diana said, "and we correspond with about ten young people our ages in India, Africa, and South America. Say, Barbara, don't you belong to something

149

like the Bob-Whites here in Iowa?"

"No," Barbara answered slowly, "but I wish we had a Bob-White club here." Then her face brightened. "I do belong to a wonderful club . . . but maybe you belong to the same one, because there are branches all over the United States, even all over the world."

Mart whistled. "Jiminy, that sounds like a big order!"

"Is it a church group?" Honey asked.

"No," Barbara answered. "It's called Four-H. Do you know about it?"

"Yes," Trixie said. "I've heard a lot about it. It's mostly for young people from farms, isn't it?"

"Not exactly," Barbara said. "Mrs. Schulz is one of the leaders. Gosh, I'm glad I'm in her group. There are twenty-two of us, an average group, I guess. I think she even sponsored a group in Evanston, didn't you, Mrs. Schulz?"

"Yes. However, Trixie, it really is mostly for young people in rural areas," Mrs. Schulz said. "Maybe because cities have playgrounds and community houses and places like that. You see, we've always lived out in the country, and we were almost in the country in Evanston. The Four-H is under the direction of the Federal Extension Service."

"What do the members do?" Jim asked politely.

"Everything under the sun," Bob answered. "Clubs can have almost any kind of project. Right now, I'm working with four others—at least five members of a club have to work on each project to make it earn

150

standard rating—on improved grain feeding for grow-ing Jersey calves."

"And my group is working on Holstein calves," Ned said.

"Wait till the Dairy Cattle Congress at Waterloo, and you'll soon find which breed is better," Bob said confidently. "It'll be Jerseys. Their milk is a lot higher in butterfat."

"Holsteins give a greater volume of milk," Ned in-sisted. "That counts, too, remember."

"*We* have a sewing project," Barbara interrupted. "This is the second pair of slacks I've made myself," she said proudly.

Honey went over to Barbara's chair for a closer look. In spite of the wealth of her family, in spite of the fact that when Honey first came to the Manor House, her clothes had come from New York and Paris, Honey loved to sew.

"Honey made all the curtains for our clubhouse back home," Trixie said, with a proud glance at her friend.

"She made our jackets, too, and cross-stitched our club initials on the back," Diana said. "Turn around, Mart, and let them see it."

"Barbara made all the Four-H emblems her group wear on their sleeves," Mrs. Schulz said. "Honey, your work is beautiful. I'd like to have you in my group." She went into the other room and brought back one of the green cloverleaf patches worn by the 4-H members. In each of the four leaves there was a white letter *H*.

"I remember those at the Westchester County Fair," Brian said. "This year I'm really going to find out more about Four-H and about the club projects."

"What does the letter *H* stand for?" Mart asked. "I mean the four letters in the green cloverleaf."

"Head, Heart, Hands, and Health," Mrs. Schulz said.

"The first *H* is for Head," Bob said, "to think, to plan, to reason."

"The second," Barbara continued, "is for Heart, to be true, to be kind, to be sympathetic."

"The third *H* is for Hands," Ned said, "to be useful, to be helpful, to be skillful."

"And the last," Mrs. Schulz said, "is for Health, to enjoy life, to resist disease, to increase efficiency."

"I guess we try to do all those things," Trixie said, "but we don't write them in detail. We have projects, too. For instance, Honey does mending for all our families and is paid five dollars a week for it."

"Trixie helps her mother with housework, and she's paid five dollars for that," Diana said.

"And I hate housework," Trixie said vehemently. "Di loves it. She does it, too, and takes care of her twin sisters and twin brothers. She gets paid five dollars for doing that."

"We do all kinds of jobs," Brian explained. "Anything we can do to earn money."

"We don't try to earn money with the things we do," Barbara said. "We do them to learn, to better ourselves, to help others."

"Oh, I should have explained," Trixie said quickly. "All the money we earn goes into a club fund, and we use it for charity."

"I'm sorry," Barbara said. "Do you have a health program?"

"We go in for all kinds of sports," Mart said. "We're outdoors practically all the time."

"I know how important health is," Mrs. Schulz said. "It makes all the rest of our Four-H work possible. When Ned was only five years old, I was stricken with polio. Because of that, since my recovery, I have made it my own project to see that as many children as possible are immunized through oral vaccination. I've canvassed every inch of this county, until now every child in it, and every young adult, has had the vaccine."

"She's done more than that," Ned said. "Just last summer, right after we moved here, Dad built the pool for Mom. It has a heater in it, and all summer long Mom has it full of kids. She has a worthwhile project going three days a week, too. The Red Cross uses our pool to teach youngsters—little ones—to swim. Mom is crazy about kids, if I am the only one she has."

"Jim will have to tell her, then," Trixie said, "about his year-round school he plans to have someday when he's through with college. It's for orphan boys."

"And where Brian, when he finishes medical school," Honey added, "is going to be the resident physician."

"And where *I*, if I have to speak for myself," Mart said, "am going to run the farm so the school can eat."

153

"Do tell us about all of it," Mrs. Schulz urged them.

"First, though," Bob said, "I'd like to hear a little about the country around where you live—and about Rip Van Winkle and the Headless Horseman and all those places Washington Irving described. . . ."

"Henry Hudson and his crew of the *Half Moon*," Ned said. "Do they still hang around the Catskills on moon-lit nights? I wish we had something like that around here."

"Come and visit us, and we'll take you all over the country next summer. Will you?" Jim urged.

"It's a deal if our folks will let us," the Hubbell twins chorused, exchanging pleased glances.

"The thing that interests me most," Trixie said, "is pirate gold. Pirates used to sail into the Hudson River for refuge after they'd pillaged ships on the high seas. They buried their gold along the shore."

"Captain Kidd did that," Ned said, excited.

"That's just what I mean," Trixie said. "And what I'm going to do someday is to find some of that treasure. Honey and I read everything we can get our hands on about Captain Kidd and his times, and *we know*," she said mysteriously, *"something that nobody else knows*. We know just where to look for that treasure."

"You do?" the twins asked breathlessly. Ned's black eyes were twice their size.

Trixie nodded. "I have a secret map," she said. She always liked an audience. Now she could imagine all of the Bob-Whites digging away at the shores of the

Hudson, digging and uncovering brassbound chests . . . and maybe a lot of admiring 4-H members watching.

"If there's any gold left in the Hudson River Valley, Trixie and Honey will find it," Diana said. "They're detectives!"

This was too much for the midwestern girl and boys. *I guess now they wish they lived in the East*, Trixie thought.

"So that's why you were so interested in my husband's black beard!" Mrs. Schulz said, smiling.

Trixie's ego collapsed like a punctured balloon. She smiled sheepishly. "It did look funny," she said in self-defense.

"Trixie doesn't make many mistakes when she's working on a case, does she, Mart?" Diana said emphatically.

Just as Mart was about to start on the story of Trixie's past exploits, the old Seth Thomas clock in the corner bonged the hour of three o'clock.

Trixie, hearing it, snapped her fingers, looked at Jim and Honey, and stood up. "I said when we came that we'd just have to eat and run," she said to Mrs. Schulz. "Now we've eaten till we almost can't run, but we have to go. I just hope we'll be in time to validate our tickets and pick up our reservations."

"We've got plenty of time—" Jim started to say, but a glance from Trixie left his sentence in midair. He shrugged his shoulders resignedly.

They found their coats and scarves, said a sincere thank-you and good-bye to Mrs. Schulz, held up their hands in a salute to the others, and went out into the rain.

"I'll run you home to pick up your car," Ned called after them. "Wait!"

"No need to do it," Trixie called back. "We'll run for it!"

Before Ned could get out of the house, they were racing toward Army Post Road.

Overboard! · 15

WHEN THEY CLIMBED into Ben's jalopy, which was parked in the driveway at Happy Valley Farm, Honey said, "I've known you to be pretty cagey at times, Trixie, but I never till today heard you say something that wasn't true."

"What are you talking about?" Trixie asked, terribly concerned.

"I mean what you said about having to go to the airport about our reservations. That isn't true, is it?"

"It is true, sis," Jim answered for Trixie. "The tickets have to be confirmed. It *could* be done by telephone—but you said you wanted to shop, too."

"Honey, you don't honestly think I'd tell a lie about

157

it, do you?" Trixie's face was very sober.

"I've never thought such a thing before," Honey insisted, "but this is the first I've heard about having to go to the airport. Do we have to go this very afternoon?"

"Not exactly . . . maybe not exactly this afternoon," Trixie admitted. "You'll remember, though, that Uncle Andrew warned us to take care of it in plenty of time. What's wrong, Honey, in doing it now?"

"Nothing, I guess," Honey conceded. "Are we really going to the airport or just to Walnut Woods?"

"Both places," Trixie said, quickly. "The airport first, aren't we, Jim?"

"That's right, Trix," Jim said and backed the car around. With a loud blast of the exhaust, they were up the road and on the highway to the airfield.

Once there, they took care of the business of tickets, browsed in the gift shop, then went back to the car.

"The rain hasn't stopped a bit," Honey said. "It was good of that man to put our tickets in a plastic envelope so they wouldn't get wet, wasn't it? It sure is pouring down! This jalopy looks even worse than Brian's."

"Yes, and with that boat on top, it's so top-heavy I have a hard time steering," Jim said. "I don't see why Ben doesn't take it off when he knows he isn't going to use it."

"If you'd look at the way he has it tied on, you wouldn't wonder," Honey said, laughing. "Right now, I think we'd be better off in a boat than in this jalopy.

158

Is that water down there in the Hubbells' field, Jim?"

"That's just what it is," Jim said. "Will you give up, Trix, and go back to Ned's house?"

"Jim Frayne, of course I won't," Trixie said. "This is the very last chance I have. I know just exactly where to look for those men. I know where I saw that light in the woods. The water isn't even near the road. Jim, you just went past Sand Hill!"

"Oh, Trixie, let me out of my agreement, won't you?" Jim said. "This is a day for ducks."

"I think we *have* to go over there today," Honey said. "It means a lot to Trixie. It should mean a lot to you, too. We want to do something for Trixie's Uncle Andrew, after all the fun we've had this week."

"Right you are, sis," Jim said. "You've heard my last word. Wait till I turn this bus around and get onto Sand Hill."

It was easier said than done. In backing around, Jim went into the ditch, and the girls had to get out and push. The mud splashed on them, and their clothing clung to them.

"You two look just like the witches in *Macbeth*," Jim said.

"I'll lend you my compact, and you can see what *you* look like," Honey said. Then, as he straightened the car, she said, "It looks like clear sailing now."

"Sailing is right," Jim agreed. "Down there on the woods road the water is almost over the shoulder. But here we go . . . kersplash!"

"It's the *first* road," Trixie directed. "We took the second one, if you'll remember, Jim, that night of the barbecue, and it's a dead-end road. It was just opposite here," she went on, "that I saw that light. Stop a minute, please, Jim!"

Jim slowed the car, and Trixie took some small field glasses from a case in her pocket.

"Gosh, you think of everything!" Jim said admiringly. "Can you see any sign of life over there?"

"Not yet," Trixie said, trying to adjust the lenses.

"Let me take a look," Jim said, and Trixie handed over the glasses.

"The woods are so dense and the rain's coming down so hard I can't see a thing," Jim said. "Wait a minute. I'll pull a little closer."

Jim started the car. The engine roared. Then a noise far louder intruded—a crash, as though a dozen brick walls had fallen.

"What's that?" Honey asked and grabbed Jim's arm.

"Darned if I know," Jim answered. "Do you have any idea, Trix?"

"I think I do . . ." Trixie said, really frightened now. "In fact, I *know* I do."

"The bridge over the Raccoon River went out!" Jim guessed.

Trixie nodded, unable to say anything.

"We'd better get out of here in a hurry, then," Jim said. "Here, take your field glasses, Trixie."

A rush and a roar of water followed the collapse of

the bridge. About fifty or seventy-five feet from them, water swirled angrily. They were now on the edge of a bayou, and, as Jim tried to start the car so that he could turn, great branches floated by out in the current, then the bloated body of a cow and half a dozen chickens.

"Turn around as fast as you can," Honey urged, terrified. "Oh, you *can't* turn around, Jim! There isn't any road!"

"It's dry land where we are," Trixie said.

"Just now it is," Jim agreed. His face was grim.

"Let's not get panicky," Trixie urged. "I'm going to have another look. I think I see something over there. Look, Jim!"

"Are you crazy, Trixie?" Jim asked exasperatedly. "Forget that house in the woods. You don't seem to realize that we're in real danger. I don't know what to do first."

"We *are* in a jam," Trixie said apologetically. "And it looks as though we're going to be in a worse one. Jim—"

"Yes, Trixie, what is it? You'd better come up with an idea."

"Let's get out and take Ben's boat off the top of the jalopy. We'll be a lot safer in a boat than we are here."

They hurriedly piled out of the car. In a few minutes Trixie said, "Quickly, Jim—there—it's loose on this side. The water's coming right up to our feet! Push the boat off, Jim! There now—*shove!*"

The little rowboat plopped into the water, and they all scrambled into it. Just in time, too, for the water, rising quickly, swirled around the car as they pushed away from it. Then, viciously, the backwash lifted the small, high, old-fashioned jalopy and carried it ten or fifteen feet, then whirled it out into midstream.

"There goes our last touch with dry land," Jim said, "and there goes Ben's pride and joy. Honey, Trixie, you take the other oar, and I'll get this one. I think—this—is—the—toughest spot we've—ever—been—in."

The girls didn't answer. They couldn't.

"Hold your oar steady, girls," Jim ordered. "We have to turn this boat. It's drifting toward the current—and—we—have—to—turn it," he panted.

The girls strained to hold the boat as nearly steady as possible. Jim tugged with his oar against the rush of water. Finally, reluctantly, the boat veered around.

"Now, pull!" Jim shouted. "Pull hard!"

"There goes a chicken house," Honey said. "I suppose all of the chickens have been drowned. Isn't this terrible?" Honey put her hands before her eyes.

"Keep pulling, sis!" Jim commanded.

"Oh, see what's on top of that chicken house," Trixie called. "Stop, Jim! Stop!"

"I will if you tell me what for," Jim said. "This isn't an outing, Trixie. We're in big trouble!"

"You *have* to stop before that chicken house gets down where we are," Trixie said. "Jim, there's a little puppy on top of it. He's crying. Hear him? Let's try

162

to work our way over to him.''

"And get hit midships with that big old hen house?"
Jim asked. "You've lost your mind, Trix."

"She has not," Honey said, pulling hard on the oar.
"We can't just let that puppy drown. Look, Jim . . . it's
a setter puppy . . . just like Reddy back home."

"Don't cry, baby!" Trixie called to the dog.

When the puppy heard her, it started yapping happily, just as though it were saying, "It's people, and
they'll know what to do."

"That does it!" Jim said. "Poor little guy. Hold your
oar firm, and I'll see if I can get any closer to the hen
house."

"It's rammed up against a tree trunk now," Trixie
reported. "Thank heaven. Now, if we row fast, we can
reach it before the current catches it and whirls it
away."

Jim, his eyes determinedly trained on the puppy and
measuring the distance they had to go to save it,
pulled harder and harder.

"Now!" he shouted triumphantly. "Jump for it, fella!"
He held his oar steady with one hand and reached for
the small puppy with the other.

Confidently, accurately, the puppy jumped. Jim
caught it by its front feet in midair and tossed it into
Trixie's lap.

"There's your puppy," he said. "I wish I were as sure
of saving *your* lives. We've got to regain the distance
we lost by backtracking. Do you see that red barn?"

Jim pointed to a barn that just barely showed its red top, far back at the beginning of the Walnut Woods road.

"I see it, Jim," Trixie said.

"That's where we have to set our sights. That's where we have to land to get away from this flood. That's Ned's father's second barn. He just bought the land. There's no house on it, but he uses the barn. Ben told me about it when we were fishing. I hope we make it!"

"We will!" Trixie said, her lips firmly set.

"We will," Honey said, just as confidently. "I've been praying—hard."

"We all have, I think," Jim said. "Don't stop now. Trixie, what in the name of heaven are you doing?"

Trixie had taken the glasses out of her pocket, and as she helped Honey row with one hand, she held the binoculars to her eyes with the other. They were trained on the woods.

"I just *have* to look," she explained. "After all we've been through—are going through—I want to take a last look to see if I can see anything over there in the woods. Jim! Jim!"

In her excitement, Trixie dropped the glasses. The puppy, startled from her lap, barked and whined.

"Sit down!" Jim commanded.

"I *am* sitting down," Trixie shouted. "Jim, I saw something! Here, I've got to look again. It *is.* I can see them plain as day! Jim, it's the thieves, as sure as you're born . . . right over there on the edge of the woods.

They're marooned with a big truck. And what do you think they have in that truck?"

"I don't know, but sit down! For the love of heaven, sit down, Trixie! I swear I'll bat you over the head with my oar and knock you down if you don't. We're in real danger, Trixie. Sit down!"

Trixie, so excited she forgot where she was, didn't even hear Jim's shouting. "It's bundles of wool!" she screamed. "That's what they have in that truck— bundles of wool! They're beckoning to us to come over. Jim, it's the thieves! It is! Oh, jiminy jeepers, hallelujah, it's the thieves! I can tell the sheriff exactly where to find them—exactly—and they can't get out! Jeepers, Jim! Here, take the glasses; look!"

Trixie, in spite of Honey's restraining hand, leaned over, and the boat tilted dangerously.

"Trixie!" Jim shouted. *"Trixie Belden! Sit down!"*

Startled, Trixie realized suddenly where she was, stumbled at Jim's sharp voice, tried to regain her balance, and fell into the river!

Deadly Danger · 16

SWIM! KEEP PADDLING!" Jim cried to Trixie. "Keep circling the boat if you can. I'll pick you up. Honey, hold it steady. Here, Trixie, here on this side!"

Trixie, her mouth full of muddy river water, paddled vigorously to keep afloat. "Don't worry," she called to Jim and Honey. "I've been overboard before!"

"Not in a current like this," Jim said. "Listen to me, Trixie. *You're in deadly danger!* Hold steady! Honey, hold that oar!"

Honey, white-faced and shocked, sat like a marble statue in the boat, never touching the oar. The puppy in her lap wiggled and whimpered, his small head against her shoulder.

166

"Honey!" Jim called. "Snap out of it!" With his oar, he dipped water and splashed it on her face. He had to have her help. Startled, Honey recovered and seized her oar.

"Keep that oar steady!" Jim said to her sternly. "Now, Trixie, now—there we are—wait a minute; don't try it now. I'll hold the boat a little closer. Now!"

Trixie, paddling hard, reached for the boat, missed, reached again, and tried to climb in on Honey's side.

"Not there!" Jim called frantically. "Can't you see I've pulled the boat around so you can get in the bow? There, now, let loose, Trixie!"

But Honey, so anxious to get Trixie back in the boat, leaned forward too far. The boat tipped, then capsized, and they were all in the water! The little puppy, terrified, paddled vigorously at Jim's side.

"Oh, Jim!" Trixie wailed. "See what I've done!"

"Keep still, both of you," Jim said. "Don't waste breath talking. Thank goodness you can swim. Hold on to that oar, Trixie. I have the other one. I'll right the boat. There! Over it goes—and the puppy into it, and the oar. Shove the other one back to me, Trixie—there—in it goes, too. Just keep afloat and swim in the direction of the shore. We have to get away from this current!"

"What will *you* do?" Trixie said. "We won't leave you."

"Trixie, just please don't talk. Do as I told you! I'll pull the boat after me and swim toward you. Don't swallow any water!"

Honey and Trixie, their clothing hampering them seriously, churned the water and, with the extra strength born of fear, managed to propel themselves slowly, surely, away from the current.

Back of them, Jim made slower progress, dragging the boat and trying to swim with one arm.

"You can wait for me now," he shouted. "Tread water if you can. When I reach you, stay on opposite sides of me. I'll try to pull the boat in between you."

Honey and Trixie splashed hard, trying to stay, as nearly as possible, in one spot. The water was a little quieter. The downpour of rain had slackened.

Once the boat slipped away from Jim, but he turned quickly and retrieved it. Literally inching his way, he finally guided the light craft between the two girls. Then he held the stern low and told Trixie to ease herself aboard.

This accomplished, he swam around to the other side and helped Honey in; then, with both girls in the stern, he clambered into the bow himself.

Exhausted, the three of them sat for a moment saying nothing. The half-drowned puppy snuggled close to Trixie for warmth, its little tongue caressing her hand.

Jim reached under the seat, opened a watertight compartment, and pulled out a bucket and a big can.

"Start bailing!" he called when he had recovered his breath. "Take turns! We're almost level with the water!"

All three bailed. It didn't take long to reduce the water load to practically nothing.

"But we're floating backward!" Trixie called frantically as she stopped bailing and looked up.

They were, indeed. Jim had forgotten, in his eagerness to ease the load of water in the boat, that the backwash could carry them toward the river.

"Grab the oar!" he called, and he seized the one on his side. "Pull hard!" he ordered them. "Pull! Trixie, what's the matter with you? Are you paralyzed?"

"I'm not," Trixie answered. "But I just thought of something."

"Forget it. Think about that red barn up there ahead —pull for it, Trixie! Come on!"

"I can't," Trixie said.

"Why not? Are you sick?"

"No, but, Jim, thieves or no thieves, those two men back there are human beings. They'll die just like all those drowned chickens and that cow, and we can't let that happen to them. We have to go back there after them."

Jim threw back his head and laughed. The sound was so strange that Trixie and Honey were speechless. Had Jim, in his desperate worry, completely lost his mind?

"How do you suppose you saw them so well through your binoculars?" Jim asked Trixie. "They're on a rocky point, well above the water."

"Then why didn't *we* try to get over where *they* are?" Trixie asked reasonably.

"Because they would have taken our boat and let us

169

do the waiting, while they escaped," Jim said. "Start rowing, Trixie."

"If . . . well, if you're sure they'll be safe," Trixie said. "We couldn't just leave them."

"They're a lot safer than we are, Trix, and a lot more comfortable," he added. "Aren't you freezing?"

"I just never thought about it," Honey said, "did you, Trixie? But I *am* cold, aren't you?"

"I just keep my eyes on that red barn," Trixie said. "If we reach there safely, then I'll take time to be cold. Anyway, this little fellow is so warm. You hold him for a while, Honey. He's like an electric pad. And, Jim—"

"Yes?"

"If those men are safe, and the road out is all covered with water, it won't be hard for Sheriff Brown to arrest them when we tell him about them, will it?"

"I guess you're right, Trix," Jim said. "I just hope we get a chance to tell him. Right now we have to pull hard for that barn. It's beginning to get dark, but, thank goodness, we're getting nearer to the shore—barn, I mean. There isn't any shore, as far as I can see."

"Over there," Honey said, holding her hand to her eyes and pointing, "snagged against that old tree. It looks like the carcass of a drowned sheep. Isn't this flood terrible?"

Trixie looked in the direction Honey pointed. "It is terrible," she said. "Something strange, though. That sheep has been shorn, and it isn't shearing season yet. Why, don't you know, that's just what those thieves have been doing: stealing Uncle Andrew's sheep, shearing them to get the wool—it was in that truck—then selling the carcasses to some of the lockers around here."

"Well," Honey said, "you weren't so far wrong, after all, Trixie, when you said that lamb we ate at the barbecue at Rivervale was stolen. I just hope that principal has a chance to eat his words—talking to Ned the way he did!"

"Please—please!" Jim said. "Row! Keep your eyes on that barn. We're gaining on it!"

The girls obeyed. They were almost completely exhausted when they edged near enough to the barn for Trixie to catch the top of a door that protruded from the water.

"Hold on tight!" Jim told her. "I'll pull the boat alongside it. We can stand on top of that door you're holding and crawl in the haymow window. There, Honey, it's on your side—steady! Step out!"

"I can't," Honey wailed. "I just can't. I'm scared to death!"

"I'll do it, Jim," Trixie said. "Sit down in the boat, Honey. There's nothing to it."

Trixie, never relaxing her hold on the top of the barn door, pulled herself to the top of it, swung herself up on the sill of the haymow window, miraculously open, and climbed through. Then she reached down, took the puppy Honey held up to her, put it through the window, and reached back to help Honey, who, a little ashamed and more confident now, climbed up

171

and into the relative safety of the haymow.

"You come in now, Jim," Trixie called down.

"I've got to try to fasten this boat some way before I leave it," Jim said. "We might need it."

"There's a chain with a rope at each end of it under the seat where I was sitting," Trixie said. "It's what Ben used to fasten the boat on top of his car."

"I saw it," Jim answered. "But what good is it? What can I fasten it to?"

"If you reach down into the water below the top of this door," Trixie answered, "you'll find some kind of a latch or bolt. I felt it with my foot when I was climbing up here. Maybe there's a hasp on it, and you can tie the rope there."

"I'll try," Jim said. "Sure thing, here it is—and it's better than a hasp—there's a staple the latch fits over. There!" he said and reached down, threaded the rope through the staple, pulled it tight, knotted it, passed the oars up through the mow window to Trixie, and, breathing heavily, joined the girls, safe in the haymow of the old red barn.

"Back there," Honey said, "I never thought we'd make it. I remembered all sorts of things—like how good my parents are to me. I wish—"

"Don't you dare say it, Honey Wheeler," Trixie said. "I wish the same thing, though," she admitted. "Moms and Dad, Bobby—"

"And Sleepyside," Jim said. "Gosh, we'd never be in this fix in Sleepyside. Trixie, I want you to know right

172

now how thankful I am to you for helping me get away from my stepfather and for helping me find my new family."

"Trixie, you've helped so many people," Honey said.

"Not any more than you have, Honey," Trixie said. "I only wish I could think of a way now to get us out of this barn and safely back to Happy Valley Farm. Nobody will *ever* think of looking for us here."

"Nobody knew we were even going to try to go to Walnut Woods," Honey said worriedly.

"It won't take Mart and Brian long to think of it," Jim said. "They know their sister, and they'll start looking for us."

"Will they ever look for us way out here in all this water?" Honey asked. "Will they even find our bodies?"

"You give me the creeps," Trixie said. "You can think of the most terrible things sometimes. Honey Wheeler, I'm ashamed of you!"

"I'm ashamed of me, too," Honey said. "Mart and Brian are your brothers, and you know them better than I do. You know if they'll think of looking for us way out here."

"If there's one thing I'm sure about with Mart," said Trixie, "it's his ability to read my mind. He'll know, somehow, that I persuaded you two to go to Walnut Woods with me. Because it's so near the time for us to go back to Sleepyside, Mart'll know that I'd never give up till I tried again."

"Isn't that the truth?" Jim said.

"I'm just as sure of this, too," Trixie told them. "*Somebody* is going to find us and save us."

Jim got up from the bale of hay where they were sitting and walked to the mow window. What he saw made him turn, trying to conceal his fright, to the girls.

"They'd better work fast," he said. "We're going to have to get out of this haymow."

Trixie hurried to the window, looked once, then said, "The water's up. It's higher—quite a little higher—since we climbed in here."

"Yes. The boat's underwater, too," Jim said. "What do we do now? I thought we'd be safe here. I guess we should have stayed in the boat." Dejected, he sat down on a bale of hay and put his head in his hands.

"We're not licked yet," Trixie said. "This isn't the highest place in the barn. There's still the roof."

"And no way to get to it," Jim said.

"I'm not so sure. Keep your chin up! You've been the one to see us through this far."

"I know when I'm licked," Jim said. "We'll just have to hope that the water doesn't come up here. We can still take to the rafters."

"No," Trixie said, "that isn't good enough. There must be some way that window closes. If there's a shutter of some kind. Or maybe a sliding window!" Trixie felt around outside the mow window as she talked. "There isn't anything out here," she said, "except some sort of a track, as though a sliding window is supposed to travel on it."

174

"Try to find the window," Honey said.

"We don't need the window!" Trixie said. "Jim, if you stand on this track—"

"Yes," Jim said, "and I pull myself up on that, stand on it, climb up there—"

"And hold on to the eaves to help us up," Trixie said.

"I'll never be able to do it," Honey said, looking up at the roof.

"I'll go after Jim," Trixie said hastily. "It'll work, Jim. Out you go!"

Jim climbed through the window, wrapped his hands around the iron bar above him, pulled himself up, stood on the bar, found a secure hold on the eaves, then slowly climbed to the roof.

Once he slipped and almost went into the water, then recovered himself and tried again.

Later, Trixie, safe on the roof, almost lost her hold when she and Jim were lifting Honey.

Those were the things they didn't dare to think about as the three of them, and the small puppy under Trixie's arm, sprawled in precarious safety on the roof of the barn.

No Place to Go · 17

GRADUALLY THE TRIO realized that, for the moment, at least, they were safe, and they looked around. The ascent of the roof from the eaves was gradual, growing less steep as it reached the apex. There an old-fashioned cupola perched.

The light had almost faded from the sky. Carefully bracing her feet against the eaves, Trixie sat up.

"I can just barely see Sand Hill," she said. "I don't believe there's any water over it yet."

"Can you see any sign of life anywhere—any automobile lights or anything?" Honey asked. She was too frightened to change her position.

Jim took the puppy from Trixie and settled him in the

curve of his own arm. His feet braced against the eaves, he surveyed the area around them. "There are cars coming and going on Army Post Road," he said. "Not a thing heading this way. I guess everyone has been warned about the flood."

"I'm pretty sure I can tell where Happy Valley Farm is," Trixie said. "The lights in the house and the floodlight in the yard seem to have been turned on. Ned's house, across the road, is a blaze of light."

"By this time, they must surely know something has happened to us," Honey said. "Trixie, will we ever—"

"Don't say it," Trixie said. "Look how high and dry we are."

"High enough in the air, I hope," Jim said, "but far from dry. I can still wring water from my clothes. It's a good thing the rain stopped."

"And a good thing we all have our jackets," Trixie said, "though I almost took mine off when we fell in the water."

"That was a horrible time," Honey said, shaking with cold and fright.

"It was," Trixie said. "But it all came out all right, thanks to Jim."

"And a certain pretty keen girl called Trixie Belden," Jim added. "Sis," he said to Honey, "please don't be frightened anymore. It's only a question of time till somebody comes after us."

"How?" Honey asked.

"Motorboat," Jim said.

"Did you see any in Trixie's uncle's yard?" Honey asked despairingly.

"No, but I saw plenty of them over on Waterworks Lake. They were still covered up and in dock for the winter."

"That doesn't do us much good here, a mile or more away," Honey said realistically. "You can't float a boat down Sand Hill."

"What's the matter with you, Honey?" Jim asked. "You're always such a good sport. How did those boats get out to the lake in the first place? Trailers, of course. There's always a way."

"There aren't any motorboats out there hunting for us now, are there, Trixie?" Honey asked. "Do you see any lights—you know—shining on the water?"

"Not yet," Trixie answered. "But we will!"

It had grown quite dark now. Stars filled the sky, and a wan moon at the edge of the horizon tried vainly to lighten the night.

There was no sound of life near them—nothing but the rush of the current in the river, far too near for comfort, and the swishing and swooshing of dislodged trees as they floated into the backwash.

Suddenly the barn shook as though from an earthquake.

Jim and Trixie quickly sprawled on the roof.

"What was that?" Honey cried, her voice shaking.

"Something hit the side of the barn, I guess," Jim said. "A chicken house or smokehouse or something

178

else that the flood carried away."

"Do you think it knocked the barn loose?" Honey asked anxiously.

"I doubt it, sis," Jim said. "It's anchored on concrete a foot thick. It's an old barn, remember, and well built. Anyway," he went on, "we're still on top of it."

"Jim," Trixie said, not listening to anything that was being said, "isn't there *some* way we can signal? So when they do start to look for us down here in the flooded district, we can give them some indication of where we are?"

"We can yell like the dickens," Jim said. "I was just going to do that."

"And we could wave my flashlight," Honey said, pulling it from deep in her pocket.

"For gosh sakes, Honey, where have you been keeping that?" Jim asked. "How did it survive your dunking in the river?"

"I forgot I had it," Honey said, ashamed. "It was buttoned into my pocket. Anyway, it was light until a little while ago. Shall I wave it around?"

"Sure thing," Jim said. "And I'll yell!"

So Honey waved and Jim yelled, and after a little while Trixie and Honey yelled. Then the puppy started to howl. He howled so vigorously that he slipped from Jim's arm and slid slowly down the roof toward the rushing torrent.

Jim made a lunge for the little fellow and caught him just as he struck the eaves.

179

"Thank goodness you got him," Honey cried. "I'd have died if we'd lost him now. Stop crying!" she told the puppy, who, more frightened than ever, yipped at the top of his voice.

"What's the matter now, Jim?" Trixie asked as she caught sight of Jim's face, grim in the dim light of the moon.

"We have to climb higher," he said. "Start climbing. Trix, you lead the way."

"What is it, Jim? Did the barn cave in when that thing hit?" Honey asked, trying to scramble after Trixie.

"No," Jim said, "it didn't, but—well, I might as well tell you. The rain may have stopped, but the river is still rising. It's up to the eaves now. Climb! We have to make it to the ridge of the roof. Get going! Faster!"

It was harder for Jim to climb, because he held the puppy in one hand. Slowly, though, they made progress. Twice Honey slipped, and Jim stopped her with the elbow of the arm that held the little dog. "Take hold of Trixie's hand!" he ordered.

"Here!" Trixie called. "I've fastened my scarf to my arm. Hold on to it, Honey. There, do you have it?"

"Yes, Trixie," Honey said faintly.

"Then hold tight!"

Arduously, feeling their way, the three Bob-Whites continued to climb.

"Say," Trixie called when she could see over the ridge of the roof, "it isn't bad at all up here. The roof sort of flattens out. It's really wonderful, Honey. It's a lot better than down there on the slant. Climb, now! You're doing fine! There!" She gave a final tug to her scarf, and Honey landed beside her.

"Why didn't we do this before?" Jim asked, surveying the wide flat space.

"For the good reason that it's a silly roof," Trixie answered. "It's all slant on this side and a big flat space on the other side. We couldn't know that."

"It's almost like the sun deck at our house," Honey said, sighing with the first sense of security she had felt since they reached the barn.

The puppy, sensing a relaxation of the tension that had kept him quivering, wiggled out of Jim's arm and started chasing his tail!

The Bob-Whites laughed, and the puppy, encouraged by their amusement, circled wider, almost fell off, and had to be rescued again.

"I know just the place for you," Jim said. "We have enough to think about, without having to save your life every five minutes. In you go!" He dropped the struggling puppy into the cage of the cupola.

"He's safe there," Trixie said.

"But what a dreadful noise!" Honey said. "Hush, little puppy! Hush! It's all for your own good."

"Let him howl!" Trixie said. "It'll save *our* voices. Jim is so hoarse he can only whisper. We'd better start signaling again, though, Honey, with your flashlight."

"Don't you see *any* sign of a boat?" Honey asked anxiously.

"Not a thing, sis," Jim said. "Keep your chin up!"

"The first thing they probably did when we didn't get back to Ned's," Trixie said, "was to go and look for us in Valley Park."

"Or the airport," Honey said. "No, probably the first thing they did was to get mad at us for not going back to the party."

"You're probably right, Honey," Jim agreed, "but that's all over now. It's about time they started out on the water route."

"Maybe the police won't let anyone on the water," Honey said.

"Maybe not," Jim said, "but the police themselves will come out and hunt for us. There are probably a lot of other people marooned."

"I don't think so," Trixie said. "There's no house around here as close to the water as this barn. It's all lowland, Ben told me, and nobody builds here or tries to raise crops. It's flooded every year."

"Not like this," Jim said, "with even the bridge out. Think of all those chicken houses and the drowned animals. Where did they come from if there aren't any people around?"

"Way up the river, maybe," Honey said. "Jim, I think my battery is getting weak. Doesn't the light look a lot dimmer to you?"

"It sure does," Jim answered. "We'd better save it till we catch sight of some boat."

"Then Honey and I had better yell again," Trixie

said. "Your voice is almost gone."

Both girls cupped their hands around their mouths and called at the top of their voices, "Help! Help! Help!"

Not a sign of anything appeared on the water. Their voices just echoed back, till finally, as hoarse as Jim, they had to give up. They could only whisper.

"What can possibly be keeping the rescuers?" Honey asked. "It must be near midnight. Of all the times for us to leave our watches at home . . . every one of us!"

"It isn't midnight," Jim said. "I'm sure of that, but I'd have thought the police would have a search party out on the water long before this."

Trixie heard the anxiety in Jim's voice. But she had something worse to worry about. No one else had seen it yet.

Water had crept up over the eaves and was slowly, but surely, rising. Trixie had noticed it about fifteen minutes before. Since then it had risen at least an inch.

There's no use telling Jim, Trixie thought. *There's nothing else we can do. There's no place else for us to go. We have to stay right here and. . . .*

She couldn't even think the word *drown*. *Why, oh, why doesn't someone come?* she asked herself desperately. *If I were back there at Happy Valley Farm, I'd know by this time that we must be out here trapped by the flood or else. . . .*

Trixie hadn't fooled Jim. That was apparent to her

183

now, when she saw his eyes turn away and look down the slanted roof.

Water seems so harmless, she thought, her mind half deadened by the shock of their growing danger. *It's just rippling away down there as it creeps higher up the shingles—rippling away—* She thought of something. "Jim!" she cried out loud. "Jim!"

"Yes, Trixie," Jim asked, "what is it?"

"There's always the top of the cupola!"

"It won't hold more than two people," Jim said.

"What are you two talking about?" Honey asked. "No one can sit or even stand on top of that cupola." Honey had been putting her fingers between the bars of the cupola, playing with the puppy's paws, resigned to wait it out till someone found them. Now she turned an anguished face toward Jim and Trixie. "After all we've been through," she said, "is there more danger?"

"I'm afraid so, sis," Jim said, his voice but a hoarse whisper. "Give me the light. I'll have to signal with it till the battery goes dead. I can't yell anymore. Neither can either of you. Trixie's voice is the worst of all."

Honey handed him the flashlight.

Both girls watched as Jim pushed the switch, waited for the light, and pushed the switch again. Finally, as he realized the battery had at last died, they saw him throw it, with an angry gesture, far out into the water.

A Sound in the Dark · 18

SOMEHOW JIM'S GESTURE of despair made Trixie angry clear through.

"See here," she said. "We just *can't* give up. Jim, I'm surprised at you. You've been so wonderful, and now you've lost heart."

"I have not, not for a single minute, Trix," Jim said. "I can get mad as well as you, can't I? That darned old flashlight!"

"You're both putting on an act," Honey said. "I can tell. How could we possibly be in a worse spot? Look out at that water. It's creeping higher and higher all the time. We're freezing cold. We're starved. We're so hoarse we can't even call for help anymore. Now the flashlight's gone. Even you can't find a bright side to the fix we're in, Trixie."

"Oh, can't I?" Trixie asked. "You listen to me, Honey Wheeler. We could easily have drowned out there when that boat turned over, but we didn't."

"What difference does it make *where* we drown?" Honey wailed.

"And furthermore," Trixie went on, "we're high up, on top of this barn. It could be pitch-dark, but the moon is giving more light all the time. We're way off from the main current of the river. Maybe the water *is* rising. Maybe it'll get higher and higher, but we're in the backwash. Even if we were in the main current, the foundation of this barn is just like rock. So pull yourself together, Honey."

"I'm sorry I'm such a goon," Honey said. "I'd like to be big and noble like you, Trixie—"

"Oh, rubbish," Trixie said. "I'm not big and noble, and you know it. I just have confidence that we're going to get out of this. Say, why don't we get our minds off the whole thing for a while? We'll all flip if we keep talking like this. Let's play Twenty Questions!"

The suggestion set Honey laughing for some reason or other. *That sounds good*, Trixie thought.

"Maybe playing a game sounds silly," she said aloud. "But let's do it, anyway. I'm thinking of something."

"Animal or mineral?" Jim asked, glad to get into the game to help take their minds off their predicament.

186

"Animal."

"Manufactured?" Honey asked.

"Yes."

"Does it belong to any one person?"

"No."

"Is it alive?" Honey questioned.

"Oh, Honey," Jim teased, "how could it be manufactured and alive? Is it edible?"

"Yes," Trixie whispered. Even her whisper was hoarse now.

"I know what it is," Honey said, tears in her voice. "It's Mrs. Schulz's fried chicken, and I'm so hungry and cold, and I'm terrified! I don't want to play any old game. I just want— Jiminy, do you see what I see? Over there toward what you said was Sand Hill?"

Trixie, who had hardly taken her eyes from the spot since darkness came, said exultantly, "Yes, Honey—oh, yes, Honey—I see it—a light—and it's coming this way. Hey!"

She tried to call. Nothing came but a hoarse croak.

Jim tried to call, too. But his voice had gone completely.

Honey tried—in vain.

Only the small dog's half-whimper, half-yip cut the silence.

"Nobody will pay any attention to the dog," Honey whispered. "How can we let them know where we are?"

Jim pulled a piece of iron loose from the cupola. When the *putt-putt-putt* of the outboard motor grew nearer, he beat hard against the hinges of the cupola windows. The noise was loud, but evidently no one in the boat heard. The frightened little dog inside the cupola cried more plaintively.

The light of the boat came nearer. "It's Mr. Gorman's flash lantern," Trixie said. "It's a boat from Happy Valley! Oh, *make* him turn that flash lantern this way! What can we do?"

In the pale light of the moon, they could see two figures in the boat.

"One of them is Mr. Gorman," Trixie said.

"The other is Mart, I think," Jim said. "If only they'd cut off that motor for a little bit, we just might be able to make them hear us somehow."

As though they had heard Jim's mind, the motor was cut off, and the boat drifted. Someone took a megaphone and called, "Jim! Jim! Trixie! Trixie! Honey! Honey!"

"It's Mart!" Honey choked.

Oh, heaven, let one of us be able to answer, Trixie prayed. Together they tried. The hoarse, frantic sounds almost burst their throats. But no one could possibly hear them.

The boat drifted nearer and nearer, near enough that they could hear the voices of the people in it.

The puppy yipped. The water in the river lapped quietly, menacingly, against the roof. Trixie tore off her jacket and waved it frantically. So did Honey. Jim beat on the iron hinge.

In the boat, Mart held the megaphone to his mouth and called, "Jim! Jim! Trixie! Trixie! Honey! Honey! Are you out there somewhere? Answer! Jim! Trixie! Honey! Trixie-e-e!"

Suddenly Trixie dropped the jacket she was waving, and, with an exultant hoarse cry, she put her two fingers to her lips and whistled shrilly: *bob, bob-white! bob, bob-white!*

Out in the boat Mart threw his arms in the air for joy, and back came the answering whistle: *bob, bob-white! bob, bob-white!*

Jim and Honey, overcome with joy, sat silent.

Off in the high water, the motorboat came alive. Its motor turned over, started up, and, straight as an arrow, came to the edge of the old red barn.

Mr. Gorman raised his gun and shot into the air.

From the far edge of the water another gun answered.

"They know you're safe," Mr. Gorman said. "Thank God!"

When the boat grounded at the foot of Sand Hill, a crowd of about fifty people waited. There were men, women, boys, and girls, even a dozen or so from the Rivervale High crowd.

Brian and Diana joyously threw their arms around the trio. Someone wrapped blankets about them. Someone else herded them into a waiting car.

Up the hill they went, with all the cars following.

189

In Trixie's arms, the puppy went to sleep.

Back at Happy Valley Farm, Mrs. Gorman waited. Immediately she took charge of the blanketed Bob-Whites. "It's into warm baths for all of you," she said. "Hank, you take Jim—"

"Holy cow," Jim said, "I can still bathe myself!"

It broke the tension. Everyone laughed, even Mrs. Gorman. Jim's big, lanky form towered above stocky Mr. Gorman.

"Heavens, I didn't mean that!" Mrs. Gorman said. "I just meant for Hank to draw the water. We want to do *something!*"

She herded Honey and Trixie ahead of her. "Heat the coffee, Diana," she called back. "As soon as they get into some dry clothes, they'll need food and lots of it . . . and then rest."

"We've been roosting up there on top of that barn so long we don't need any rest," Jim said, "but, oh, boy, dry clothes and food!"

"Someone give the little puppy some warm milk, please," Trixie said. "We found him out in the river, floating on a chicken house."

"Come on, Moses," Mart said and picked up the puppy.

"That's a perfect name for him," Diana said, laughing and crying at the same time. *"Moses!"*

When the castaways finally came down to the kitchen, Mrs. Gorman had banished everyone except

Ned and the Hubbell twins. They all sat around the big kitchen table, everyone talking at once.

"What took you so long to come after us?" Honey asked.

"We didn't think about the boat on top of Ben's car," Mart said. "We were hunting for you in the jalopy. We thought—let's not talk about it, shall we?"

"All right," Trixie said. "Then I'll tell *you* something mighty important." She described the two men she had seen on the high point near the woods, the truck filled with bundles of wool, and the shorn sheep's carcass that had floated near them.

"Then you really did see a light off in the woods," Mr. Gorman said. "I didn't believe it could possibly be true at first, but you were so sure. I told the police about it today when I went to Valley Park. Sheriff Brown just laughed at me. I'll go call him. He won't laugh now."

"The worst thing about all of it," Jim said, "is losing Ben's jalopy."

"Well, gosh, Jim," Ben said, "if you think I'd ever give that a thought. . . ."

"When my daddy and mother hear about what almost happened to us," Honey said, "they'll get Ben the finest car to be found in the city of Des Moines."

"Wouldn't I look funny in a fine car?" Ben said.

"Trixie's Uncle Andrew will replace Ben's car," Mr. Gorman said. "When I think of how I've made fun of him for keeping that boat on top of his car! He ought to get the Carnegie medal for keeping it there," Mr. Gorman added vehemently.

"Amen!" Trixie said. "Oh, Ben, how glad we were to have that boat when the bridge went out!"

"A boat's a handy thing," Ben said. "Say, where is it now?"

"Fastened to the window on the haymow of the red barn," Trixie said. "It's underwater now. Ben, when you get your new car, there's going to be a new boat fastened on top of it, if we have to dip into Bob-White funds to get it. When I think of what might have happened. . . ."

"Don't!" Mrs. Gorman begged.

"Well, Gumshoe Trixie tracked down the sheep thieves, after all," Mart said. "Belden and Wheeler, private detectives, always get their man!"

Somehow, no one felt like laughing. Even Mart couldn't enjoy his attempted joke. The price of Trixie's triumph this time had been almost too high.

The Missing Clue · 19

IT WAS LATE when Jim came up to the house and Trixie and Honey came into the kitchen the next morning, Saturday. Trixie was the latest of all.

She found the kitchen in an uproar. Moses was barking as the kittens spat at him. The kittens won, and Moses retired to shelter behind the big cookstove.

"That puppy should have been named Jeremiah," Mr. Gorman said. "He wailed all night. Didn't you hear him?"

"I couldn't have heard Gabriel blow his horn last night," Trixie said. "Poor little puppy. He was lonesome. I should have taken him up to my room."

"He isn't lonesome anymore," Mrs. Gorman said as

she put a plate of steaming pancakes in front of Trixie. "Ben has adopted him—unless, of course, we find his owner. He says he's going to make a hunting dog out of him. He will, too. Moses is a fine puppy, and Ben can train any animal. He's even taught squirrels to climb up on his shoulder to find nuts in his pocket."

"Ben's awfully nice not to have made a fuss about his car and boat. He loved that old jalopy. Mr. Gorman, did the sheriff go out after those men on the point?"

"Yes," Mr. Gorman answered. "Took them to Valley Park and put them in jail there. That jail itself ought to cure them of sheep-stealing."

"I'm sure sorry that I got Honey and Jim into so much danger," Trixie said, shaking her head, "but it *is* a good thing to have that mystery about Uncle Andrew's lost sheep solved, isn't it?"

"It would be if we were sure that it's solved," Mr. Gorman said. "It's no cut-and-dried case."

"What do you mean? The men came from back there in the woods, where they were hiding. They had a truck full of wool. No one keeps sheep back in those woods."

"They claim they bought the wool over in Warren County. The sheriff isn't too sure they didn't. They're making a big fuss about being kept in jail. Sheriff Brown says he has no right to detain them for more than the rest of this day."

"Oh, Mr. Gorman, that's terrible," Trixie said and got up from the table, leaving her food untouched.

194

"I'm *sure* they're the ones who stole the sheep."

"I have a feeling they are, too, Trixie, but that's not proving it. Sheriff Brown says they asked him how on earth they could get away with all those sheep, right in plain sight, with the dogs around."

"They have a point there," Mrs. Gorman said. "Don't worry, Trixie. Sit down and finish your breakfast. Right's right."

Trixie tried to eat but couldn't. To come so near to a solution! To be so sure she was right! Something in the back of her mind bothered her. She felt there was some clue, somewhere, that she had missed. What could it be?

Mrs. Gorman let the kittens out into the yard, and Tip and Tag came racing into the house. They caught sight of the new puppy and rolled him around with their paws, nuzzling him.

Suddenly Trixie snapped her fingers. Something in the dogs' play sparked her memory. "Where's Jim?" she asked.

"In the next room," Mrs. Gorman said, "looking at the newspaper with Honey. Why do you ask?"

"No reason," Trixie said. "I'll just go and talk to them for a while."

In the living room, Trixie huddled with Honey and Jim. There was the sound of low voices talking fast. Then Trixie and Honey streaked upstairs, put on their jackets, and were downstairs and out the door with Jim, like lightning.

195

Tip and Tag ran after them and around them and ahead of them, barking, sniffing the ground, sniffing the air, so glad to have someone to walk with.

"I remembered the dogs," Trixie said, "and the way they acted down there in the corner of the field when we were hunting jackrabbits."

"With the sheep bunched in the corner," Honey said.

"Yes, and they scattered when we made so much noise. They seemed to have found something *very* attractive down in that corner. And there are a lot of sheep over there right now," Trixie said.

"They look as though they were hunting something," Jim said. "Something may grow there that they particularly like to eat. Hey, Trixie, what is it?"

"Something they like to eat, all right," Trixie said, "but it doesn't grow here. See here, Jim!"

Trixie held up a long pan. Sticking to it were the remains of some mixed grain mash. Not far from it was another pan just like it—and another.

"No one would ever carry warm mash this far out in the field, away from the barn, would they?" Trixie asked.

"I don't think so," Honey said slowly. "Trixie, do you see all those bunches of wool on the fence?"

"I see something worse than that," Trixie said. "I see big patches of what must be dried blood . . . there on the fence and here on the grass. If it hadn't rained so hard, I could tell better."

"Someone has been luring the sheep down here with

mash and then killing them," Jim said.

"Isn't that terrible?" Honey asked. "The poor things. The thieves must have dragged them under the fence."

"Of course," Trixie said. "That's where those tufts of wool on the barbed wire came from."

"I guess that'll convince the sheriff," Jim said confidently. "We'd better get back and let him know before he releases those prisoners and we lose them."

"How can we prove that it was *those* men who stole the sheep?" Trixie asked. "We know that *someone* did, and we know how they did it, and we're sure in our own minds that it was those men in jail at Valley Park. But how can we prove it?"

"I guess you're right, Trix," Jim said. "We're right back where we started from, aren't we?"

"Not quite," Trixie said. "Not quite. We'll just have to hunt around and see if we can find something that will connect those particular men with the crime."

"Wheel tracks of their truck?" Honey said excitedly. "Let's crawl under the fence."

Jim held the lower fence wire while the girls rolled under; then Trixie held it for him.

"They couldn't have picked a better place to get away with their crime," Trixie said. "This far corner is practically on Army Post Road. They didn't even need to run their truck up onto the soft ground and leave tracks. No, there's not a thing here."

Honey, kicking around in the stubble, struck something with her foot. She pushed it over in front of Jim.

"It's a knife," she said, "a heavy one. Sort of a sharp knife, isn't it? It's just beginning to rust . . . can't have been here very long."

Trixie bent over it. "Are there any marks on it?"

Jim turned it over and over in his hands, then handed it to Trixie. "Not a thing I can find," he said. "It looks like any other knife to me. Maybe you can find something on it."

Trixie looked, then sorrowfully gave it to Honey. "Hold on to it," she said. "If there ever was a mark—a fingerprint or anything like that—we've destroyed it by handling it. If anyone finds anything else, for goodness' sake, let it stay where it is till we can pick it up by the corner with a handkerchief."

"It doesn't look as though there's going to be anything else to pick up," Jim said, disgusted. "I should have remembered fingerprints."

"Honey and I will make wonderful detectives if we can't remember an elementary thing like that," Trixie said.

Jim laughed. "Do you know what Mart would say if he were here and heard you say that?"

"No," Trixie said. "What?"

" 'Elementary, my dear Watson,' " Jim said. "He's always calling you a 'female Sherlock Holmes' and Honey 'Dr. Watson.' "

"I wish I really were Sherlock Holmes for about half an hour," Trixie said. "What's that thing you're squashing under your foot?"

Jim moved his boot.

"Some kind of an old hat," he said and picked it up.

"Pick it up by the corner!" Honey cried.

"Don't worry," Jim said. "Fingerprints wouldn't show on an old hat like this."

"A name on the sweatband *would* show," Trixie said. "Let me see."

Jim turned the crown of the old battered hat inside out, and there, inked in durable black on the sweatband of the hat, were the initials R.M.

"Jeepers!" Trixie said. "Gosh! Now, if those just happen to be the initials of one of those men! Did either of you hear Mr. Gorman say their names?"

"I didn't," Jim said.

"Neither did I," Honey answered.

"Then let's find out," Trixie shouted.

As fast as they could run, the three Bob-Whites dashed down Army Post Road, turned in at Happy Valley Farm, and burst into the kitchen, waving the old battered hat.

"What on earth?" Mrs. Gorman gasped.

"What's the excitement?" Mart and Brian and Diana wanted to know.

"Call Mr. Gorman in from the barn!" Trixie begged. "Somebody, quick!"

Mrs. Gorman stepped outside the door and beat on the triangle hanging there. Mr. Gorman and Ben both came running from the barn.

"Call the sheriff, Mr. Gorman," Trixie said, the words

falling over one another. "Ask him the names of the prisoners—hurry!"

"What in the name of common sense—" Mr. Gorman began.

"Don't lecture, Hank," Mrs. Gorman said quietly. "Just call the sheriff and do as Trixie asks."

"What's it all about?" Mart asked. "Spill it, somebody."

"Why all the melodrama?" Brian asked. "Tell us, Trixie."

Trixie didn't answer. She couldn't. She was too excited. She just pointed to Mr. Gorman and the telephone.

It seemed to her that it took ages for him to dial the number. She could hear the sound of ringing. *Will he ever answer?* she thought.

"Hello! Sheriff? Hank Gorman speaking. Say, Joe, what are the names of those men you picked up on the point? . . . Yes, the ones with the truckload of wool. . . . What did you say? . . . Jake Burton?"

Trixie's heart hit the ground.

"And the other one? . . . Yes? . . . Oh, yes, I hear you . . . Rancy Miller."

Trixie and Jim and Honey began to dance around the room singing "Glory, Glory Hallelujah!" at the tops of their voices.

Mr. Gorman waved frantically, trying to quiet them.

"Wait," he said to the sheriff on the telephone. "Hold on a minute till I talk to these crazy hyenas." He held the receiver to his chest and consulted with Trixie, smiled, and turned back to the telephone. "What do their names prove?" he said. "Well, they mean just this: These kids have found some evidence that the men you are holding are the thieves we've been after. It's plain as two and two makes four. Yes . . . sure, hold on to them. We'll be in Valley Park in a jiffy. They're the culprits, all right. Good-bye, Joe!"

Trixie Scores Again · 20

TRIXIE, JIM, HONEY, Brian, Diana, and Mart climbed into the big yellow Happy Valley Farm station wagon and headed for the village of Valley Park. Mr. Gorman drove, and Ben went along.

As they turned and drove to Ned's house, they honked, and Ned came running. When he found out what had happened, he wanted to go with them. Later, down the road, they picked up the Hubbell twins at their house.

As they passed Sand Hill, Trixie looked toward the place where the big red barn stood. The water was just beginning to recede. From the middle of the stagnant backwash, though, just a small part of the roof and the cupola still protruded.

Trixie shivered and moved closer to Jim. He put his arm across the seat back of her. "Don't even think about it, Trix," he said. "We're all safe now, and over there in Valley Park are the thieves you've been after."

"I know that, Jim, and I'm not thinking exactly about myself. I never should have taken chances with your life and Honey's," Trixie said. "I just hope my parents don't forbid me ever to do any more detective work."

"I'm not sure I'd care a lot if they did," Jim said.

"Why, Jim!" Trixie said, shocked. "What if someone should tell you that you shouldn't have your school for boys that you've planned ever since your uncle's money was left to you? What if someone did that?"

"It's not the same at all," Jim said. "Having a year-round school for boys is not dangerous. I hate to think of my sister and my—well, you, Trixie, getting into such tight places all the time."

When they got into town, they discovered that the flood had been the worst in the history of Polk County. A squad of men had been working all day burying dead animals. Townspeople had been out in boats since dawn, bringing in people who were stranded. Fortunately, there were no fatalities, but temporary homes had to be found for families in flooded areas.

"It's mostly people who live upriver," the sheriff told them when they went into the courthouse. "There hasn't been such high water for years, and I guess some of those people upriver thought it just never would happen again—poor souls."

"They've found out now," Ben said. "That Raccoon River is a dangerous one. I know three kids who'll say 'amen' to that."

"They never should have gone down to the woods at all," the sheriff said.

"Well, now, we've gone into all that back at the farm. Maybe they should have stayed out of the woods. But if they had, the men you're holding never would have been caught."

"Eventually they would have been," the sheriff said.

"Maybe," Mr. Gorman said. "By that time, Andrew Belden wouldn't have had any sheep left. Bring the ornery *hombres* out, Joe."

Sheriff Joe Brown sent two of his deputies to bring the men into his office. When they came in, they were defiant. "It's our word against a bunch of kids," Rancy Miller said.

"Not quite, Rancy," Sheriff Brown said and showed him the battered hat and the knife. "Found them and all the rest of the evidence back there in the corner of the Belden field," he said. "Here, Hank, sign this warrant for their arrest." He spread the paper out on his desk, and Mr. Gorman signed it in the name of Andrew Belden.

When the prisoners saw the hat and the knife, they seemed to give up. When asked how the sheep had been stolen without detection, they said they had watched till the dogs were taken into the house at dinner time. Then, between that time and the time the dogs were let out at bedtime, they got in their work.

"How did you ever get back there in the woods?" the sheriff asked. "After the road ends, it's nothing but a jungle."

"Did you ever think of following the river edge around the point and going in from that side?" Rancy Miller snarled. "We cut our way through the brush. There's a little old log house back there . . . an old still, too. If you'd let us alone, we'd have had *it* going."

"There's more goes on back there in the woods than you know," Jake Burton, the other thief, added.

The two men confessed to stealing sheep not only from Happy Valley Farm but also from half a dozen other farms in three surrounding counties. They would shear the sheep for the wool, slaughter them, and sell the carcasses to owners of frozen-food lockers.

"Then it *was* stolen lamb we ate at the barbecue!" Trixie said triumphantly.

"There's a reward out for their capture," the sheriff said as the prisoners were led out of his office. "I'd think it should be awarded to the two girls and the lad who tracked them down."

"If there *is* any reward," Trixie said, "I think the money should go toward Ben's new car and boat, don't you, Honey? Jim?"

They agreed heartily. Their spirits were so high that they would have agreed to anything. Outside, when the group climbed into the station wagon, they saw that a crowd had gathered, cheering and waving.

"You'd think we were heroes or something," Mart said.

"See, Trixie," Brian said. "You said he'd be taking some of the credit when it was all over."

"I don't want any credit for anything," Trixie said. "Anyway, Mart looked like the biggest hero in all the world to me when he came after us in that boat with Mr. Gorman."

"Back to the farm now," Mr. Gorman said.

"We *have* to do a little shopping first," Trixie said. "I want to find something to take to Bobby."

"He's crazy for a real glove and a hardball," Mart said.

"My twin sisters will want dolls," Diana said. "I saw some Indian dolls in a window. I'll get Indian suits for my twin brothers. Mrs. Gorman has given us jam for our mothers."

"We can't take very much on the plane," Jim said. "We'll have an hour between planes at the airport in Chicago, anyway. Let's go."

It was late afternoon when the yellow station wagon sped along Army Post Road, back to Happy Valley Farm. There they found the yard full of cars and a crowd of cheering young people.

The word of their peril and rescue had gone out far and wide. Now the word of the capture of the thieves had been added.

Dot was there. All the rest of the gang they had met at the skating rink were there. It seemed as though all the members of the Rivervale High basketball team were there—even the coach.

"You ran us out last night, Mrs. Gorman," one of the boys said, "but we're going to stick around now. We don't have heroes and heroines around here every day."

Trixie and Honey, overwhelmed, clung close to Jim, who just stood there, looking self-conscious. "Heck, we didn't do anything except save our hides," he said.

"*And* track down the thieves," Mart said proudly.

"Tell us all about it!" a red-faced man said, pushing his way through the crowd. "I'm from the *Des Moines Register and Tribune*," he said. "I've got a photographer here— Mike! Over here! Get some pictures of them. Half a dozen," the reporter said. "One of the puppy in Trixie's arms. Get pictures of *all* the kids from New York. Now the Gormans. Oh, come on, Mrs. Gorman, who cares if you're wearing an apron? And Ben . . . where's Ben? There, Ben, Mike'll take you with the collies."

Ben rebelled. He strode off across the field, Tip and Tag yelping after him, past a bunch of bleating sheep. Mike, not to be discouraged, fitted a telephoto lens on his camera and got a picture of Ben and the sheep.

"That's good," the reporter said. "I wanted the sheep, anyway. They're what started the whole thing. Now, kids, tell me all about it."

Trixie, Honey, and Jim, despite their protests, had

207

to tell the story of their hours on and in the water. Then the reporter got the details of the search that led to the capture of Jake Burton and Rancy Miller.

"Wait till you read it in the paper," Mr. Gorman said when the press car had driven away. "You'll never recognize it. He'll make it sound like the Israelites crossing the Red Sea."

Eventually the crowd thinned out. Mrs. Gorman extended her dinner to include Ned and the Hubbell twins. Later, happily visiting, the Bob-Whites forgot all about the time. The hour grew late. They were to take the plane at nine o'clock in the morning. Not one of them had even thought of packing. The record player was going. The television set was turned on. Tip and Tag and the red setter puppy, Moses, were running around the room, pushing and tumbling one another. Even the kittens and Blackie joined the fun on this final evening of the visit.

In their chairs by the fireplace, Mr. and Mrs Gorman watched and smiled. "It's been far too quiet in this house with no young people around," Mrs. Gorman said to Honey, who, breathless from dancing, dropped into a chair beside her. "We wish you didn't have to go back. Look at Ben! Trixie is teaching him to dance. What in the world is that outlandish thing they're doing?"

"That's the very latest thing," Honey said. "And Ben's a neat dancer!"

"He's needed livening up, too," Mrs. Gorman said.

"You've been good for him—all of you. He works too hard and then studies half the night. The Bob-Whites are the best thing that ever happened to Happy Valley Farm!"

Gradually the records became softer and sweeter, and the television programs narrowed down to the late show. After a few subtle words from Mrs. Gorman about the need to pack, Ned and the Hubbell twins left. They promised, though, to be at the airport in the morning, when the Bob-Whites took off for home.

"Don't forget to write our names and addresses in your address books just as soon as you get home!" Trixie said. "Don't forget to send us that material about Four-H work!"

"Don't forget you're coming to visit us next summer!" Mart called from the doorway as the trio left and crawled into Ned's little red car.

"Maybe our parents'll let us drive to visit you," Ned said. "I've been as far as St. Louis with my car. I think my dad just might let me drive to Sleepyside. Don't be surprised next June if you see us coming down Glen Road to Crabapple Farm!"

"Jeepers!" Trixie said. "Imagine!"

Back in the house, Mr. Gorman let the dogs out for the night and took his lantern for a last look at the big farm before going to bed. Trixie stood beside him and looked out into the dark, listening to the night noises. "It's beautiful here," she said softly. "I'll run out and see the little black lamb and the horses before I go tomorrow. The lamb's going to be all right now, isn't it, Mr. Gorman?"

"Yes, Trixie," Mr. Gorman said. "And all the rest of the sheep, too, thanks to you."

The Bob-Whites were still lingering in the living room when Mr. Gorman came in from the barn. They hated to start the job of packing.

Suddenly the sharp ringing of the telephone brought them all to their feet.

Mr. Gorman glanced at his watch. "Who in thunder," he said, "would be calling at twelve o'clock at night?"

"Take up the receiver and see," Mrs. Gorman suggested with a smile.

Mr. Gorman did just that, then turned to the group, his eyes popping. "It's Glasgow, Scotland, calling!" he said. "It's Andy Belden!"

They gathered close to the telephone, waited while it sputtered and crackled, and finally heard the sound of Uncle Andrew's voice.

"Say, this is a surprise," Mr. Gorman boomed. "Everything's going just fine. . . . No, not a sheep missing for days, and there *won't* be. . . . Sure! Your detective niece tracked them down. Honestly! . . . I'm telling the truth. . . . It was this way— Do I have time to tell you?"

Uncle Andrew must have said yes, for Mr. Gorman

told him the whole story. Then he handed the receiver to Trixie. "He wants to talk to you," he said.

"Of *course* we're all right," Trixie said. "No, we didn't count on getting caught in the flood. Everything's fine now. . . . Yes, it is, really! We wanted to catch the thieves to try and pay you back a little for the grand time we've had here. . . . Oh, Uncle Andrew, that'll be super wonderful!"

Trixie turned to the rest of the Bob-Whites. "He's going to bring us all cashmere sweaters from Scotland! . . . Yes, Uncle Andrew, I guess we'd better say good-bye. I never talked across the ocean before in my whole life! . . . Yes, I'll tell Ben he's to have the car you bought in England in place of his jalopy. . . . We did hate that! . . . Uncle Andrew, Ben heard me, and he's dancing a jig. . . . Good-bye, now. We're leaving early in the morning. Then we'll count the days till you're back in the United States and visit all of us at Sleepyside. Dear, dear Uncle Andrew, good-bye!"

The next morning, the big yellow station wagon from Happy Valley Farm deposited six happy, laughing Bob-Whites at the airport in Des Moines. They hardly had time to weigh their luggage and hurry out to the waiting plane.

From the steps, they waved to Ned, Barbara, and Bob and to the Gormans and Ben; then they vanished inside.

Trixie settled in the seat beside Jim. Across the aisle sat Brian and Honey, in front of them Mart and Diana.

211

FASTEN YOUR SEAT BELTS the light in front flashed. Trixie and Jim obeyed. Then, as the big ship sped down the runway to take off, Jim pulled a little package from his pocket. "It's for you, Trixie," he said. "I got it in Valley Park yesterday."

Trixie opened the box. She stared at the dainty silver identification bracelet that nestled there. "It has your name on it, Jim," she said and smiled shyly at him. "Put it on for me, will you?"

"You know what it means, don't you?" Jim asked.

"Tell me," Trixie answered.

"It means that you're my special girl, Trixie," Jim said. "As if you didn't know that already."

The plane lifted. The landscape below grew smaller. Blue sky and clouds surrounded them.

Trixie looked happily at her bracelet, then reached over and put her small, sturdy hand into Jim's. He closed his long fingers tightly over it. With a sigh of complete happiness, Trixie settled back contentedly.